THE GEEK

Novels by Craig Nova

TURKEY HASH
THE GEEK
INCANDESCENCE
THE GOOD SON
THE CONGRESSMAN'S DAUGHTER
TORNADO ALLEY

THE GEEK
CRAIG NOVA

A Delta Book
Published by
Dell Publishing
a division of
Bantam Doubleday Dell Publishing Group, Inc.
666 Fifth Avenue
New York, New York 10103

ISBN: 0-385-29718-1

Reprinted by arrangement with the author

Printed in the United States of America

Published simultaneously in Canada

10 9 8 7 6 5 4 3 2 1

May 1989

BG

For Ruth

1
The Girl
and the Jackass

Boot found the girl on the beach: hair and one arm animated by slight waves, her water-soaked dress ripped enough to expose adolescent breasts, an untried stomach, perfectly formed limbs. There was a neat line of holes that ran diagonally across her side and lower stomach. Each perforation was surrounded by darkened flesh. A sand crab, its movements abrupt and mechanical, crawled slowly between the girl's legs, toward furrowed flesh, a slightly flaring ridge of hair.

There was a disease on the mainland so similar to plague as to inspire the same fear, and at night there were those who tried to flee to the island, risking the patrol boats that worked in the channel between dusk and dawn. From the sea the island looked brownish and rocky, projecting in startled relief above blue water, the mountain ridges appearing serpentine, as though the island were some buoyant lizard, both fantastic and forbidding. There was a leper colony at

3

one end, but the lepers were confined to their grounds and were rarely seen in the streets of the village, although every now and then children clowned, pulled hands into stumpy claws. The patrol boats were armed with machine guns.

The fisherman said, "What?"

Boot stood in the door of the fisherman's lean-to. The fisherman held a glass of ouzo.

The fisherman was called Petros and he lived alone. All the fishermen on the island were superstitious, but Petros was more so than the others. He took his boat at night and watched the stars, listened as the fish filled the nets. His beliefs were a dam against terror, since there were times when he acted in a manner that confused and frightened him. Some islanders argued that the boils caused the episodes of generic idiocy. Others said it was the ironing. Because when Petros was four his scalp flowered, bloomed with sores that itched and were crusted and oozed a yellowish substance. Petros' father, a fisherman who was almost as superstitious as the man his son became, went each day to the monastery and prayed and lit candles before the ikons, but the sores continued to ooze. So, after two weeks, he rowed (which shows that the islanders' lives had improved some in fifty years, because now Petros had an inboard engine) to the other side of the island, taking with him his wife and Petros to see the sorceress, who looked at the head and scraped off some of the crust and put it in a sack for safekeeping and advised the use of a poultice and heat. Petros' father gave her a coin, rowed back to the lean-to, and made the poultice and waited, and the sores grew worse. Petros' father said to his wife, Bring the iron. The wife brought the iron, one that had a lid and required coals for heat, and his father put in the coals and the mother held Petros and covered his head with a cloth and his father ironed the boils and waited again, and this time, whether the disease had run its natural course, or because the heat had dried up the sources of infection, the boils disappeared.

But soon Petros' father was back at the monastery and back to see the sorceress as well, because Petros acted like an idiot. And when Petros became an adolescent he masturbated so much that his father bound Petros' hands with tape. Petros' father went back to the sorceress, who made a tea from the crust of the original sores. Petros drank the tea, but it did no good, certainly less good than the tape, which worked except for those times Petros was alone with his younger sister, who had the compassion to remove the tape and leave him alone in the bushes.

Boot heard the arguments in tavernas.

There's no need. Because if you have parents stupid enough to iron your head the chances of getting a full deck are pretty slim anyway.

But time helped. When his father died, Petros was more than capable of looking after himself: the stupidity had been relegated to periodic fits, seasonal ravings. And when these episodes were barely noticeable, or when they had been accepted by the islanders as part of their own heritage, Petros married a woman who was twenty years older, ugly and old and with a small dowry, because Petros was a poor fisherman who lived in a lean-to and who had a reputation for stupidity. Everyone was ashamed at the wedding, but shame didn't keep guests from getting drunk on the liquor of the bride's parents, nor did it keep them from making jokes about the match that could be heard by everyone. The bride's dowry was just enough to pay for the inboard engine, but on the night of the wedding the engine hadn't been bought, so Petros' bride had to put the stumbling, shamed Petros into his boat (the same one that his father had used) and row him to the lean-to and then coax him from the boat into bed.

The wife lived for fifteen years. She died so quietly that Petros slept next to the corpse for eight hours before taking notice of her death, and then spent the next ten years alone, fishing, drinking in a taverna, always sleeping on his side of the bed, becoming surprised at how much his mind cleared as the years passed. And although his superstition and religion were stronger than his father's had been, when Petros was fifty years old, about the time Boot came to live in a house near the lean-to, he had developed a certain slyness.

"Bring your boat," said Boot.

"It's bad luck to carry a body in a boat," said Petros.

Boot waited on the beach, flicking away with a piece of bamboo that had been growing near the shore the sand fleas and crabs that hopped and crawled around the girl. The half-foot waves broke with the same insistence as an unfastened shutter beating against the side of a house in a strong wind. Petros stood in the center of the boat, using the oars like stilts. The inboard was always saved for longer trips.

"What are you doing?" said Petros.

Boot held the bamboo as though it were a fishing pole. The girl lay beneath the pointed leaves.

"Nothing," said Boot, throwing the pole into the water.

Petros beached his boat and stared at the girl.

"Give me a piece of cloth," said Boot, pointing to one of the burlap sacks that Petros used to carry his catch from the boat to the fishmongers.

"There's no hurry," said Petros.

Boot took a piece of cloth and covered the girl.

"I won't take it," said Petros.

Boot dug in his pockets for money.

"No," said Petros. "It's bad luck to carry a body in a boat. I won't do it."

"All right," said Boot. "I'll keep the sack."

Boot's house was at the base of one ridge that formed with another a small valley, about a hundred yards long and a hundred and fifty yards wide. In addition to Boot's house there were four other structures: a farmer's house, a taverna that was open two days a week, a church that was maintained by Petros and had been maintained by Petros' father before him, and Petros' lean-to. Sometimes fishermen who were caught in bad weather spent the night in the church, a small round building covered with plaster, topped with a dome and a cross. There were fields, small rectangular plots that ran from Boot's house down to the beach, banked there by a stone wall. Some of the smallest plots were planted with tomatoes and squash, but the largest and best pieces of land were planted with grapes: at least there was a little money in wine.

After a while, when the land is cut up some more, one man, finally, will have just enough to bury himself in one six-by-nine patch planted with vines and squash. But fishermen have it easier.

He still held the note over the girl.

No one divides up the ocean for a daughter's dowry. A fisherman can throw himself in anywhere and call it good.

Two farmers worked in the fields, a man and a woman, both old and almost indistinguishable from each other because they were of the same size, height, and weight, and they held their clothes in common, sometimes picking up in the morning what the other had discarded the night before. They lived in a house that was on the same ridge as Boot's, but it was a little farther up, connected to the fields by switchbacks cut into rock. They worked the land with

7

short-handled hoes, stooping over the vines. From a distance each looked like some man-size growth on which someone had put a straw hat, a hat that would serve better in compost than on someone's head. The hoes chopped into black mounds as the farmers directed water into one row at a time.

But the land was farmed scientifically, or could have been farmed scientifically if there had been money to follow modern advice: twice a year a man came from the department of agriculture to look at the fields and to talk about poisons and fertilizers, and since he was a lecher of almost legendary (and therefore almost acceptable) proportions, to inspect the island's crop of daughters as well, his remarks concerning which were almost as important as those concerning the squash or vines or irrigation systems. He didn't come as often as he used to, since the farmers were long past the age of bearing children.

There was nothing the farmers could do about scorpions: they were drawn to water.

"I need to borrow your jackass," said Boot.

"He won't take her," said Ulla, looking up, squinting into the morning sun.

"Is it bad luck to carry a body on a jackass?" said Boot.

"It's bad on a boat," said the man, who didn't bother to look up or break stride, still using his hoe in an old and easy motion.

The woman began to use her hoe again, striking in counterpoint to her husband. Boot knew that as soon as he was over the ridge the woman would be in the harness of the boom, where the jackass was now, turning around the well to bring up water.

"And the pack saddle," said Boot.

"It's in front of the house," said the man. "In the shade."

The scorpion, jointed, green, shiny, came from under a leaf of the squash vines.

"Give me the razor," said the farmer.

His wife took the razor from her apron, and the farmer slashed the rising sting and sucked blood. Boot stepped on the scorpion, feeling the tender shell crack beneath his heel. The farmer spit onto the green leaves.

"If you keep him overnight," said the farmer, "you've got to feed him."

That would be two days she'd have to turn the boom.

Boot unharnessed the jackass and cinched up the pack saddle. The cinch was homemade, braided from bits and pieces of worn rope. On the beach Boot lifted the girl, smelled the salt and seaweed, and turned toward the jackass, trying not to touch the girl's flesh, holding her by the dress alone. Flies buzzed on the beach. The dress ripped and the girl fell onto the pebbles again, now completely naked, sprawled, obscene. Boot took his pocketknife and slit the burlap sack near the bottom: he didn't want to make an opening for the head, but he was afraid the sack wouldn't cover the girl unless he did. He propped her up and dressed her in burlap, working it under her buttocks and over her thighs, covering the exposed groin. The jackass stood quietly, watching Boot with a blunt indifference. Boot put the girl sideways between the two X-shaped saddletrees, then carefully tucked her hair into the ragged collar and covered her head with the water-soaked dress.

"Here," said Ulla, the farmer, holding a piece of rope. She stood on the stone wall at the end of her field. "You'll need this."

Boot wrapped the rope over the girl and under the trees. He cut a piece from one end and tied the girl's legs together at the ankles. She lay face down on the jackass.

"He wouldn't take her," said Boot.

"So," said the woman.

"Maybe I'll only take her as far as the monastery," said Boot.

The monastery was halfway to town.

The jackass knew the way because the woman's son, who lived in town, used the animal to pack in warm beer and ouzo for the taverna he kept open two days a week. It was a place where fishermen came, or perhaps some villagers on an outing, but whether they were fishermen or villagers, they usually came by boat. The island had been shelled heavily during the war, and every now and then someone was killed by stepping on an unexploded shell. The road was safe enough, but it was half a mile from Boot's house to the road.

The girl amplified the movement of the jackass as it picked its way among the stones. Small, quick lizards, the color of artichokes, raced among the rocks as Boot followed the jackass to the top of the ridge.

Shit. I didn't bring water.

He looked at the bay, the land around it shaped like two fingers about to pick up a pin, the water so clear that Boot could see the stones on the bottom, the submarine vegetation covering them. The jackass's hooves clicked on the stones that lay in the path, which was bordered on both sides by desertlike plants. The dirt road appeared to Boot as a whitish excoriation in the side of hills that dropped to the sea.

The road began just beyond the opium smuggler's yard, on both sides of which were low buildings that looked more like animal sheds than places where people lived, huts that seemed to grow from the ground itself, since they were constructed of the stones that covered the landscape. The opium smuggler slept in the road, or at that point where his yard turned into the road. He slept in the morning sunlight, using his dog for a pillow. The opium smuggler had black hair and a graying beard, a reddish face, a posture that was at ease anywhere, a mercenary eye: he had a reputation for getting what he wanted. It was founded on dealings so delicate and so crude that no one on the island really knew how he went about succeeding. Since most islanders held success, any kind at all, in awesome appreciation, the opium smuggler's dealings had become part of the islanders' mythology. He terrified most people. When the engineers had come with bulldozers to extend the road from the monastery to the cove where Boot lived, the opium smuggler erected a barricade and stood in the sunlight, swilling liquor and holding a breech-loading rifle that his father had wielded in fantasies of defending the island against hordes of invading Turks. The opium smuggler swore that any man who touched a machine would be feeding vultures before dark: the rotting carcass would be a monument to the foolishness of trying to build a road through his yard. He swore in a manner so blasphemous that grown men were frightened by it. The engineers asked permission to return to town.

The opium smuggler swore whenever he came from his house and saw that the road entered the outer part of his yard.

"If people want to buy opium," said the opium smuggler, "they don't need roads."

The house Boot rented was available because of the opium smuggler, since no one wanted to pass him or his yard or house on the way to town. Boot and the opium smuggler got along well, though: Boot never came around after dark, liked to smoke a little opium now and then, liked to drink, and liked to listen to stories. And he had enough sense not to ask any questions, aside from those about the language, which the opium smuggler answered freely, giving obscene examples. It didn't bother the opium smuggler that Boot was a foreigner, since the opium smuggler himself was something of an alien on his own island: he had no friends, only business connections.

There were stories told on the island of the disappearance of young women, of screams and cries coming from one of the low buildings near the opium smuggler's house, of hurried, predawn crossings in a small boat to the mainland. The opium smuggler was asleep in the road because he was drunk, and he was drunk because business was bad: the disease made it doubly difficult to make the channel crossing, whether just for opium or as a private trading route, young women one way, opium the other.

After six months, after watching Boot carefully, the opium smuggler said, "You know, my life would be a lot easier if I could find someone to grow it on the island."

He said it and stared at Boot, and Boot nodded.

"You understand," said the opium smuggler.

"Yes," said Boot.

Because that was the one thing the opium smuggler had never been able to arrange. The land was too valuable, not in dollars, but in generations of toil and frustration. It was the emblem of marriage as well, since for centuries a piece of land had been the basis of any respectable dowry. It was too personal a substance to defile by the growth of opium. So the opium smuggler continued to make the crossings of the channel, knowing that even if he found someone who would be willing to grow it on the island, the crop would have to be cultivated in secrecy, for fear other farmers would come to burn the fields.

The jackass scattered chickens like the bow of a boat spreading waves. Boot squatted next to the opium smuggler and waited for him to open an eye. The dog wagged its tail, then ran to the jackass and began to sniff. Boot threw a stone and the dog howled and ran toward one of the buildings that looked like a henhouse.

"What's on the jackass?" said the opium smuggler.

"I need water," said Boot. "I'm going to town."

The opium smuggler looked at the well-formed limbs and thick hair with an appraiser's eye. He knocked pale dust from the American T-shirt that Boot had given to him.

"You can see what's on the jackass," said Boot.

Boot took the bottle that was lying next to the opium smuggler and drank twice, swallowing quickly.

"It would be all right to drink my liquor," said the opium smuggler, "if you bought opium. But you don't buy opium anymore."

Boot shrugged and pulled on the bottle, feeling his stomach quake, tasting the licorice-tinted vomit as it climbed in his throat.

"You haven't got any," said Boot, gesturing with the bottle toward the mainland, disease.

"I'll get the water," said the opium smuggler.

He staggered once, as though it were possible to bump into a hangover.

There were bored (or previously bored: withdrawal kept them occupied) men who sat in the tavernas, too old or arthritic to work, bent as though years were heavy, men who now had running noses and whose moist eyes were set on the strait: they were short two daily pipes and getting

13

jumpy. It wasn't regret for those on the mainland that set their skittish expressions.

From a five-gallon can with the top cut off, the opium smuggler poured cool water from the well over the girl. The jackass was terrified and confused. The load didn't give and no one had poured water on the animal before.

"Have fun drinking out of it," said the opium smuggler. "It's all I've got."

The opium smuggler poured the last of the water into a small can, one that also had a lip like a saw blade, and handed it to Boot.

Water dripped from the girl's legs and arms and from the jackass's furry belly onto the road, turning the dust on the stones into thin mud.

"I need a hat," said Boot. He felt the sun on his head with an intensity equal to the sensation of the liquor in his stomach. A blob moved slowly at the top of his constricted shadow. The opium smuggler took the bottle and wiped the lip with the end of the T-shirt.

"You can never be too careful," said Boot.

"If you know so much about it," said the opium smuggler, "why are you leading this jackass around? Here." He took from his back pocket a straw hat, one that had been folded twice, and put it over Boot's head: the slowly moving blob became sharp and pointed.

"You could put some in a jug," said Boot.

"What?" said the opium smuggler.

Boot watched the pointed shadow slide over the stones. The opium smuggler was gone, or left behind, sitting at the beginning of the road, under a tree now, where there was a little shade. Boot watched the shadow, not wanting to look over his shoulder at what followed on the jackass, not wanting to look ahead because there were only the hills and the scratch in them, the road that appeared to be paved with bones. The sea seemed to be covered by a clear membrane, touched with abrasions here and there by the wind. There were hook-shaped lines attached to a fisherman's nets, and streaks that reminded Boot of the minute stretch marks women have on their breasts and hips. The jackass grazed at the side of the road, pulling at the rough growth there. Boot grabbed the halter. He drank from the can, spit on white stones, stained them with watery blood.

He could have put some in a jug. I didn't want the whole bottle.

Boot watched his shadow run down to rocks that looked newly formed, as though they had slipped that day in a molten state from the hills to the sea. The water bubbled and turned white around them, making the rocks seem not only rigid, but hot as well. Boot thought again, and grabbed the halter, and followed his shadow up the road. *Maybe he believes that only a foreigner could be brutal enough to make it possible to grow opium on the island. Maybe that's why he wants me to arrange it.*

On the left, above the road, there were terraced, almost oriental fields, each growing a large crop of weeds. The monastery was on the right side of the road, built on the top of stone that dropped as straight as curtains to the sea. It was surrounded by a wall two stories high and six feet thick. The monks' cells were on the inside of the wall, and they were connected by a veranda. The cells had only one window and one door, and these faced the church: there was nothing else for the monks to look at. There was a terrace, too, covered with flagstone, in the center of which was a large tree. Its exposed roots gripped a thin layer of soil. The terrace served as the monastery's taverna, and it had a view of the strait and the mainland.

The monastery was cool and damp. Moss grew on the walls. There were other buildings as well, but they were no longer in use, storerooms, small additions to the main wall in which, years before, monks had labored over looms and made candles and shoes and habits. The storerooms had been stocked against plague time, those periods when for years the monastery would be totally self-sufficient, as isolated from the rest of the island as a colony of lepers. But there weren't many monks left, only four now, and they depended upon the central church for support, but the amount dwindled each year, and the mainstay of the monastery had become the profits from its taverna.

Boot left the jackass in the yard, beneath a tree outside the gates, and walked to the terrace, where there were tables and chairs. He took a seat close to a retaining wall that marked the abrupt end of the stone on which the monastery was built. Below, at the bottom of the cliff, there were the remains of a medieval dock, constructed of stone and patched with cement, and still in use, both as a dock and as a platform for sunbathers. There was a woman there now, alone, nude, sunning herself and diving every now and then into the cool water.

"A foreigner," said Lukas, the monk, the one who had been elected to wait on tables.

The monk had lost at cards.

She swam gracefully, leaving behind a milky wake.

"Drinks," said Boot.

Lukas' face was set deeply in his habit, but Boot could see the pale eyes, white and patchy beard, shocked brows, fishbelly skin.

"Do you have any money today?" said Lukas.

16

Boot showed a bank note, a piece of paper covered with rust-colored ink, the same bill he had held over the girl. The day before, the opium smuggler had changed for Boot (at a rate slightly higher than the bank's) a hundred dollars into local currency: it was the last of Boot's cash (although there was still a little money), but he had been on Samos for a year and the tens and twenties looked ridiculous. The opium smuggler needed dollars.

"I'll bring beer," said Lukas. "It's too early for ouzo."

"Bring beer," said Boot, "and ouzo, too."

Boot looked at the low doorways of the monastery: the people were short, subsisting on olives, onions, oil, and bread. The island was small, and it demanded of those who lived there proportional size. There are limitations, in any case, on the engineering of flesh and bone, because a man could grow, at most, to twenty-seven feet. Beyond that the body would collapse, bones would bend and snap, flesh would sag: the whole mess would sink into a sanguine puddle.

"I was in Florida once," said Lukas.

Boot poured the clear liquid into a glass, sucked at the rim, chased it with beer, and looked down at the woman, who was pulling herself onto the small quay, being careful about her knees on the stone.

"And I learned some English there," said Lukas.

"What did they teach you?" said Boot.

"Motherfucker," said Lukas. "Horseshit. Bastard."

Boot began to laugh as he poured himself another drink. The monk laughed, too.

The woman's body was jeweled with drops of water.

"Pretty funny," said Lukas.

Boot nodded.

"You have blood on your lips and chin," said Lukas.

Boot listened to the sound of hard soles on ancient stone as he walked around the church, under the hibiscus and stunted pine, drinking from the bottle, wincing when he came into a patch of sunlight.

"The monastery burned down once," said Lukas, still sitting at the table, his voice filling the courtyard.

In the church Boot smelled the musk of centuries, the residue of a million sticks of incense. The ikons were covered with gold, and they hung on walls in which Boot could see pieces of pagan temples, columns that were used log-cabin style, one cemented on top of another. Nothing was ever wasted: churches were built on the old sites, were resonant with human sacrifice, libations. Ancient columns supported the domed ceiling, too. Petros was kneeling beneath the nave, swaying in a holy tick. Boot sat in one of the wooden chairs that were built against three walls of the church, and drank and listened to the mumbling. Petros finished, lit a brownish, crude candle, and walked from ikon to ikon. His lips made a smacking sound as they touched each one.

"I have it on a jackass," said Boot.

Petros glanced at him once, but he didn't break stride between ikons.

Goddamn sun. The door of the church swung slowly on its hinges. *Goddamn.* The light was so clear, so intense, it seemed as unchangeable as a stone.

"The monastery was very rich then," said the monk. "Centuries ago. People came from hundreds of kilometers to bring silver and gold for ikons."

Boot looked over the wall: she was dressing now, cheerfully wiggling into her clothes. He stood on his shadow, fixed there, struck by a tremor so strong his body felt like iron, stood there and watched hair twirl in sunlight, the natural and unassuming grace with which she bent over a sandal.

"Very rich," said Lukas, "and when it burned, the silver and the gold melted and ran toward the ocean, and farmers came for years with rope and hung over the cliff looking for concealed bits."

"Who is she?" said Boot.

"A foreigner," said Lukas with skoptic indifference. "Look what drink does to you."

"It's not drink," said Boot.

"You don't have to get angry," said Lukas.

"I'm not angry," said Boot.

The monk's face was swallowed by the habit. Boot drank from the bottle. The woman wore a pair of jeans and a blouse and had a scarf around wet hair. Boot watched her climb the switchback that led from the ancient quay to the monastery terrace, noticed that she took an obvious joy in walking, in the shock of working flesh. When she stepped onto the terrace Boot could smell the sea on her skin. He still wore the opium smuggler's hat, carried the bottle and the can with the ragged lip, had blood on his lower face.

"Hello," Boot said in English.

"Hello," she said, and walked through the monastery to the gate, carrying over her shoulder in a cheerful manner a bag which held a towel and a brush. Boot was already at the gate, there in time to see her look at the jackass, at what was on it: she gave Boot one horrified glance and began to run up the road.

The monk stood at the gate, too, and looked at the jackass tethered in the yard. Boot heard an engine turning over, the harsh sound of grinding gears, tires spinning in gravel. Boot stood with the bottle, astonished, smelling the silty odor that drifted into the flat and shaded place in front of the monastery.

"She had a car," said Boot.

"A little red one," said Lukas. "With the top down."

The monk looked at the jackass, at what was lashed onto it, and said, "It doesn't matter. She wouldn't have taken it anyway."

The monk checked the rope that held the girl, retied it with experienced hands, then brought from the monastery a bucket of water and poured it over the girl.

As though she were a fish, as though it were air that killed her.

Boot smelled the silty dust, watched it settle on the trees and road, the jackass and the girl.

"It's the drink," said Lukas, but he looked at the blank rock in front of the monastery when he spoke.

Boot stood with the bottle, looking at the jackass, reaching for the sloppy, loose lips.

"Petros said you'd leave it here," said Lukas.

"You don't understand," said Boot.

"Here," said Lukas.

He gave Boot his change, a blue bill, half the original, a lot of money for one beer and one bottle of ouzo.

"Isn't there any more change?" said Boot.

"I have to pack in liquor," said Lukas.

The monk filled the can with the jagged lip, left it on the ground, and was gone, and Boot was watching the road, looking for the imprint of treads. At the top of the hill, beyond the terraced fields, there was a radar tower with a metal flower rotating at the top. Boot squatted at the side of the road, drinking alternately from the can and the bottle, tasting blood. The jackass was grazing, standing over the shadow of a cross. Boot saw Petros' boat moving toward the town, the white wake of the prop looking like smoke beneath the water.

He'll tell them, and they'll be waiting.

He grabbed the lead rope and saw that the girl's dress was no longer wrapped around her head. The road was empty, without sharp color, a pile of cloth. There was some dry grass at the side of the road, and Boot tried that, grabbed a fistful and spread the bleached stalks over the girl's head, but the grass fell away, made the girl that much more insulted, demeaned by the shoddiness of the attempt. Boot pulled the bits of grass from her hair, then covered it with the opium smuggler's hat. The jackass turned with a quick grabbing movement to nibble at the side of the road.

"Go way," said Boot.

He pushed the jackass's head, picked up the lead rope, and walked again, drinking, squinting now into the sun when he put his head back. Olive trees undulated softly in a light wind, the silver undersides of the leaves cutting the dull landscape.

I know that Lukas dreams of virginal thighs, of a hymen tearing with the sound of a ripping sheet, the monk coming gold, as though the sun itself ran from his body, waking to frustration and holy disgust, semen on the cot, a shaking hand before the ikon. I understand now: money isn't simply stuff that changes hands, bits of paper and metal that can be put in a sock or under the mattress or in a cookie jar, each bill and coin charged by the agony of getting and keeping it. It's more like electricity, and you've got to be careful about it.

Boot pulled away from the wetness on the road, the acidic fluid. Some dribbled on his chin and shirt. The animal grazed. Boot wiped his lips with the back of his hand and walked, then remembered the animal and the girl and went back for the rope.

21

It looks like I caught her in a hat.

He passed no one on the road, not even when he came to the paved section which was not far from the houses, plaster buildings with windows delineated by bright paint on the casements, usually green or blue, so bright they seemed fantastic, like carnival leavings. The houses were close to the road, since they had been built long before most people on the island dreamed of pavement and asphalt, of cars and jeeps, of anything aside from jackasses and goats that required only a path, and since there was no danger in a path, there was no need to be very far away from it. Now people slept uneasily, afraid that an army jeep would crash through plaster and stone. Boot felt as though he were walking in an open-air hall. There were no shadows: the midday sunlight filled the street as though light had been cut from a quarry. The jackass's hooves struck the pavement with an irritating regularity. After the turn Boot saw the village spread around the island's natural harbor, the high-tide mark of houses, shops, and tavernas.

It was siesta, but every house had its shutters open, a sign that few people were sleeping: the houses had thick walls and cool interiors, and open shutters let in the heat and the flies. Boot didn't feel the sharp edges of the can; it looked as though he had been eating flesh. Blood dripped onto his shirt, the dried vomit there. He grabbed the rope and walked toward the waterfront, where he could see some men under the awning of a taverna, Petros' boat in the harbor among some others, and farther up, in front of the hotel, the only good one in the village, or on the island for that matter, a red sports car with the top down.

Let them get hopping mad.

The car was so crimson in the noon light that the waterfront seemed wounded. The jackass's hooves cut the silence of the street. Boot thought of a sun-struck body beneath a sheet washed and dried in open air.

The old houses that lined the first part of the waterfront were covered with a yellow wash, and they had iron verandas, tall, shuttered windows, elaborate masonry along flat eaves, and they wore pocks like medals, marks from the war: men had been killed in rooms they had never seen before. They chose these houses because the walls were good and thick. The owners refused to have the pocks smoothed over because they were proud of them, proud, too, although they would never admit it, of the number of men who had died where they now lived. One on the stairway, one in the parlor, one in the master bedroom: there were bloodstains on absorbent plaster.

The jackass stood with hind feet in the gutter, forefeet on the curb, between a Renault and a Skoda. Boot stood next to the sea wall, watching boats that bucked like badly made kites. Nets were spread on the wall to dry. The bottle was almost empty: Boot stared at it with a drunk's awe of ullage.

He walked to the other side of the street and tied the jackass to the awning of the taverna and took a seat. The other men under the canopy were fishermen, a farmer, insomniac shopkeepers. They played backgammon and drank lemonade and Coca-Cola. The boy who waited on Boot was afraid to look at the blood on Boot's face, the vomit on his shirt, the jackass tethered to the awning. He stared at his shoes as he walked between tables, then at his order pad as he stood before Boot.

"Cold beer," said Boot, "and ouzo."

The boy walked to the kitchen, more frightened than before, afraid to look at his father, the taverna owner, because he had been afraid to look at Boot.

23

"Don't worry, boy," said Boot, when the beer and ouzo had been put on his table. "Everything's all right."

One of the shopkeepers was Costas, son of farmers, poor people who worked the land. They had had three children: one died, one still farmed the land, and Costas owned a shop, a place where he had been sent as a boy of eleven because Costas had been better than his father at figuring the profit (rarely) or loss (less rarely) on each crop that was produced on the farm. It wasn't one farm in one place, but plots of land scattered over the island. They were scattered by the nature of their acquisition, generations of dowries. Costas' father saw the ability with figures, and then heard Costas, at ten, explaining that the land should be consolidated, which would make it unnecessary for Costas' father to spend the majority of the day riding his jackass from one end of the island to the other, visiting each small section of land, and then moving to the next patch, a mile or so away. The father said, "Just listen to him. He wants to sell the land and buy other land. He isn't a farmer, he's a shopkeeper."

He took Costas the next morning to the shop that Costas now owned and said to the man who owned it then, "I don't have a farmer. I have a shopkeeper for a son." The father made a gesture of contempt. "He counts and he wants to sell the land. Can you imagine. Land that I know as well as my prick." The shopkeeper poured the farmer a drink, and the farmer had it in one draught and said, "Keep him, and he'll make you money. Twice a year, send me a piece of cloth or rope or a bucket, whatever you think he's worth as a moneymaker. Maybe cigarettes if he's good enough." The shopkeeper said he would send cigarettes, and Costas' father said, "Good," because he had lived in a house that burned down one night and the sorceress had told him to smoke cigarettes to get used to fire again. Costas' father walked out of the shop and went back to his fields thinking that some woman, generations before, had jumped the fence and slept with a Turk.

Costas looked at the array of objects in the shop and said to the shopkeeper, "Can I have a quarter of whatever I make beyond what you make now?" and the shopkeeper beat Costas until he saw bright lights. Costas went to work anyway, taking inventory, making orders, catching thieves, doing the books, showing profits, small ones to be sure, but profits nevertheless, and the shopkeeper cuffed Costas some more, out of spite if for no other reason. In the third year, after sending Costas' father a pail of cigarettes that was worth one hundredth of what Costas had made, the shopkeeper saw Costas staring at him and said, "What do you want, another beating?" and Costas said, "No. I want one-half of all the profits above and beyond what you made before I came. Because now it's been three years," and the shopkeeper reached to strike him, but stopped and stared at Costas and said, "You're the one who's going to own my shop."

So it was accomplished in ten years—or thirteen, counting the time Costas earned nothing aside from the cigarettes or cloth that were sent to his father. When the shopkeeper died, Costas not only owned the shop but held notes for the shopkeeper's food bills for two years, and some notes for outright loans. So Costas didn't go to the funeral: he opened the shop and took from the iron box the notes for the food and the cash and looked at them and said, "The mother-fucker. He didn't live long enough for me to make up in interest the profits from the first three years."

Costas took a wife with a clubfoot because he didn't like mobility and taught her to make change and short counts and put her in the front of the shop, and then sat on a stool in the rear, talking to people who came to trade, still catching a thief every now and then, always calculating the meager profits the shop yielded, becoming increasingly frustrated with his growing age and inability to squeeze anything more from his goods. So when he caught his son reading books and looking at maps, and when he was appalled at the mistakes the son made in changing bills, he said to his wife, "That's not a shopkeeper, that's an immigrant." The wife sat in the front of the store near the cash register and said, "You were always bitter." Costas shrugged, waited until the boy was fourteen, gave him what amounted to fifty dollars, and sent him to the capital.

Costas sat in the back of his shop and spent the afternoons in the taverna with Petros and the taverna owner, Pavlos, a distant cousin who had come to the village at about the same time as Costas, and who had acquired the taverna in about the same manner as Costas had acquired the shop, although Pavlos had had an easier time of it since the original taverna owner had been a drunk. The taking had been easier, but the beatings had been worse.

Giorgos, a farmer, came to drink, too, since he had small pieces of land on either side of the village and had to pass the taverna every afternoon. One day when Boot and the opium smuggler had been drinking, the opium smuggler said of Giorgos, He's an old fart and he's lost his wife. But he has a she-goat and I saw him tie it to an olive tree and fuck it. There are some things I'm respected for and one of them is keeping my mouth shut, so there are only three people who know about it, Giorgos, me, and you.

The dice clicked on the backgammon board. The fishermen and shopkeepers looked at Boot, who mumbled to the jackass and threw off the beer in one draught.

There was a station wagon parked at the curb, a Renault, and it was filled with almost everything that could be found in the shops of the village, although the inventory was necessarily less. The Renault had no paint; the sun and weather had long since taken care of that, and now the car was covered with a layer of rust, a ferrous skin that was the same color as the reddish soil of the island. The owner was called Thymos, and he was short and lean, a middle-aged man who toured the villages (if a loose collection of farms and a taverna can be called a village) away from the harbor, selling his wares to those who didn't have the time to come to town. He was a notorious gossip, or more than a gossip, since he was the mainstay of news. So his stories, which were never exaggerated or improved upon, were as much a part of his trade as the thread and needles, potatoes and tin buckets he sold to isolated farmers: people bought a dime's worth of aspirin to hear a word about friends, acquaintances, enemies. Thymos was no fool: the more one bought, the more one heard. So his gossiping was accepted as any other necessity, and no one minded the questions he asked, the plain digging for information, nor did anyone expect him to withhold damaging or embarrassing facts, since these were usually the most interesting. He sat now with Costas, Pavlos, and Petros: the taverna was always a good place to pick up a piece of information.

"You have no respect," said Petros.

Boot sipped ouzo.

The square, just back from the quay, was quiet. Even the cigarette kiosk was closed. Every object stood in its own shadow.

"Maybe the sand crabs and flies were more pious," said Boot without looking up.

"What happened to her dress?" said a fisherman. "Have you been looking at her?"

Boot sipped ouzo. The fishermen and shopkeepers walked toward the jackass. Costas pulled off the opium smuggler's hat, fingered the long, heavy hair.

"What happened to her dress?" said Costas.

Boot shrugged and turned up empty hands.

A fisherman hit him, knocking him toward the jackass. Boot felt chips break off a tooth at the back of his mouth.

The table was overturned; liquor ran in the gutter. Boot leaned against the fender of a parked car and picked the bottle up by its neck. *My eye, too. What am I going to look like when I get to the hotel.* The shady place under the awning, the fishermen and shopkeepers, the boy, seemed shocked into immobility. Boot spit a small chip from one of the back teeth, and then with a careful motion, as though he were paid to do it eight hours a day, six days a week, he broke the bottle on the curb. It looked like a large, transparent flower. The sun made the edges seem icy. He was on the ground again, rolling, kicking, pursued now by two of them: he squirmed under the jackass, saw for a moment dark hair hanging down the animal's side. Someone swung a chair, but it hit the jackass, and then the animal was off, frightened, running down the empty street parallel to the quay, passing parked cars, the nets spread to dry, the boats that bobbed and swayed at their anchors.

The fishermen and shopkeepers were running, too, moving down the empty street on their stunted legs. They pushed fat chests into the weak wind of their own locomotion.

Boot sat in the gutter and said, "Right in the chops."

"What?" said the boy.

He was no longer afraid to look at Boot.

"Does your father have a bicycle?" said Boot.

Boot dropped the bottleneck into the gutter. The boy hesitated.

"It's in the alley," said the boy.

The bicycle had balloon tires, handlebars that weren't just rusted, but were rust with friction-tape handle grips, a seat covered with cardboard. There was a wire basket, too. "The chain comes off," said the boy.

Boot was standing on the pedals, pumping hard, making the balloon-tired, awkward, undignified bicycle move faster than it had in years: he raced after the men. The jackass was almost unresolvable. It was terrified and fed up, and it ran to escape the town, the men in it, and the burden on its back. Groceries, the coal seller's, the cobbler's, the book and stationery store, passed in a quickened smear. The shops formed a wall just back from the water, as though it were a rampart or defense rather than the contiguous sites of money grubbing. They were filled with paper, casks of wine, new plastic tubs, tinware and cheap forks and knives, lanterns and jugs of kerosene, dried fruit, a bewildering conglomeration of objects that jarred against the flatness of the harbor.

Boot strained in the heat and alcohol, approached the men. The shopkeepers and farmers hadn't run for years, not since the war anyway, and they seemed surprised by their own exertion: red faces, sudden perspiration, noticeable hearts. The fishermen ran in front, because they at least had to row boats and take in nets. A shopkeeper swerved from the course set by the others, stumbled, then gave up all pretense, took out a handkerchief, and sat in the gutter, sides heaving, perspiration dripping from the tip of his nose.

Boot could still see the animal, the bouncing burlap sack with the limbs sticking out on one side, and over the creaking of the bicycle and his own strained breathing he could hear the distant click of hooves on asphalt. The bicycle sounded in the deserted street like a spinning wheel in an empty house.

The merchants and fishermen were stretched out like runners in a marathon race. The leaders seemed no longer interested in the jackass but in running itself, racing those with whom they usually drank lemonade and Coca-Cola.

Behind the main street, the quay, there were others, smaller and narrower, one crossing another more than once, forming a pattern that could have been taken from a nest of snakes: it had taken Boot about a month to find his way around, even though the village wasn't very large. There were shops on the back streets, too, but they were smaller than those on the waterfront and less prosperous, being farther away from the crowds of people who came to shop. The waterfront was like a sieve: it caught the largest chunks of money.

The runners thought Boot had been knocked cold in the gutter, or if awake, consoling himself with ouzo. Now they saw him pumping the bicycle, weaving from side to side, his face and its glazed slash, his eye rising into a bluish and pink lump, his filthy shirttails flapping in the wind.

The jackass turned into a side street, probably because it was the one where it always turned when it came to town to carry warm beer and ouzo for the taverna.

"Go up that way," screamed Boot, steering with one hand, pointing with the other to a side street just before the one into which the jackass had turned. The fishermen, having been given a quick and reasonable order, even though it came from a man they had been beating a few moments before, turned without breaking stride into the street Boot had indicated. Boot stopped and waited for the others and sent them up the next street, and pedaled quickly to the third, slamming on the brakes, putting one foot on the ground, and skidding into a narrow, cluttered alley, leaving a comma-shaped smear of rubber on the pavement. He slid into the trash cans that lined the far wall. Crashing tin broke the lazy silence of the alley. Boot flipped over the handlebars and hit the wall. The bicycle turned an awkward cartwheel.

Boot heard hooves in the next street, one that ran parallel to the waterfront. There were fishheads, tripe, newspapers, scallion ends, melon rinds, rotten eggplants, and other pieces of garbage in the cans, and they were spread over the ground and on Boot's shirt, neck, and face. A shutter opened above Boot's head.

"It's siesta."

But Boot was already up, pulling the bicycle from the cans, not even looking to see if it had been damaged, already mounting it, throwing one leg over the cardboard seat. He pedaled over the lids and up the alley toward a cross street, another narrow corridor of cobblestones and plaster walls in which he could hear shouts and the clicking of hooves.

The bicycle wobbled, and it was covered with garbage: eggplant, fishtails, and wet newspapers clung to the front wheel, the center post, the handlebars. The shreds of eggplant looked like small triangular flags. Bits of trash fell to the street, but a great deal stuck to the bicycle.

Boot slid around the corner, marked the cobblestones, and ran into the jackass.

Goddamn.

The jackass was skidding, too, now terrified even beyond what Boot had thought possible.

Even the garbage is chasing him.

The shopkeepers and fishermen were beating garbage-can

lids together: perhaps it was the heat, the chase, and the anger, but in any case they simply didn't know what else to do: it looked as though they were chasing a tiger out of the bushes.

Boot said, "Stop the banging."

The animal stood in a pose that lingered from the sliding stop, head down, ears drooping, eyes glazed so sharply they looked like pieces of black marble. The shopkeepers and farmers stopped banging the lids and stared with growing astonishment at Boot, the garbage, the bicycle.

"That's my bike," said Pavlos.

On the opposite side of the street a shopkeeper opened his doors, probably in an attempt to catch some of the early trade, those people who went out to do their marketing before the end of siesta. It was an all-purpose shop, one that carried a little of everything, pots, pans, tin forks and spoons, lanterns and wicks, plastic tubs, nets, spears, a little of everything crammed into a long and narrow store. Objects hung on nails driven into the walls and from hooks screwed into the ceiling: it looked as though the shop and everything in it were in suspended free fall. The shopkeeper looked at his more well-to-do colleagues, who stood in the street with garbage-can lids, at Boot, who seemed to be what they were chasing—something hatched and nurtured and escaped from a garbage can—and finally at the jackass, the girl.

The animal turned, looked at the men with the tin lids, and ran at full speed, faster than when it had been running on the quay, up the shopkeeper's steps. The girl's head and feet struck the narrow doorframe: the head made a dull sound. The shopkeeper had simply vanished, had moved into his shop as quickly as the animal and maybe even a little quicker, since he went before it, clawing the air, screaming, hooting, desperate about his wares, especially a new glass case in which there were knives, both pocket and carving, knives with bone handles and shiny blades. Boot heard the crashing sound before he reached the doorway, the sound of pails and tin lamps and lanterns falling from the walls as the jackass, convinced now that in addition to men with tin lids it was being pursued by pots and pans and lanterns and plastic tubs, too, closed its eyes and pushed more deeply into the store.

"For the love of God!" screamed the shopkeeper.

Boot swung into the store, holding on to the doorframe, and saw the jackass kicking and bucking, striking the glass counter, smashing it, throwing the prized knives among the bolts of cloth, canteens, and life jackets.

Costas, Petros, Pavlos, and the other shopkeepers and fishermen pushed inside, passed Boot as though there were something to be done, then stood in the threatening and animate debris: it looked as if they had come to the tag end of a rummage sale.

Boot ran around the corner, along the side of the store. The street was near the end of the village, and from it the barren hills could be seen. There was a large church farther up, and another building run under the church's auspices, a home for old people: the aged were already singing. Boot ran to the shop's rear entrance, a broad wooden door, one that was cracked and splintered and covered with a bright wash.

"Stop that banging," said someone from a second-story window on the opposite side of the street. "It's siesta."

But Boot continued banging, tried to pry the door open with his fingers, kicked at the wood, and ran back to the shop's entrance, hearing through plaster walls the kicking jackass, the crashing goods. He was bewildered by the damage that had taken place in the short time he had been gone: the store no longer seemed to be in free fall but in abrupt stasis. Boot looked through the debris until he found a crowbar, ran back to the door and pried off each hinge, and then fell backward, because he didn't have time to pull the door into the street, didn't have time for anything aside from his squirming retreat. The jackass pushed the door on top of Boot and ran, still carrying the girl, toward the church, the building where the old people were singing. The jackass turned right at the corner and disappeared, leaving only the diminishing sound of hooves striking the cobblestones of the back street.

At least that one's straight.

Boot pushed the brightly painted door from his legs and walked to the thin but slowly growing line of shade next to the wall. *It's straight and it runs out to the coast. So I can have a rest.*

There were shouts in the shop, an unholy swearing. Boot sat in the shade and listened to the angry voices, the hysterical sifting of broken goods. The owner of a small taverna heard the voices and, thinking that angry men need drinks, opened his doors and put out the first table, seeing the broken door but not Boot, since Boot sat where the lazy wife of the shopkeeper usually left a pile of garbage. There was some more wailing and a chorus of grumbled and aloof condolences. Boot pulled himself onto the first chair of the taverna, fingered the shreds of garbage, threw an unrecognizable section of fish to an alley cat.

It will be bad even if we catch the animal. The girl. Because we'll look foolish, and men can't stand to be foolish in their killing or in the evidence of it: a dead girl on a terrified jackass.

"Beer," said Boot, "and a shot."

The shopkeepers and fishermen filed over the broken door, kicking broken lamps, bent pails, bits of glass before them, each still carrying a trash-can lid.

Boot brushed the garbage off his clothes, leaving patches of dampness on the cloth: it looked like a large snail had been climbing over him.

"That way," said Boot, pointing to the street the jackass had entered. "Out toward the coast."

"Does someone have a gun?" said Petros.

"I do," said a shopkeeper.

"Then get it," said Petros.

"No," said Boot. "She's turning in harness now."

The fishermen and shopkeepers dropped the tin lids. A voice said, "Stop that banging. It's siesta."

"Siesta, siesta," said Costas. He made the island's open-handed gesture of contempt. "We could get another."

Boot stared at him.

"No," said Boot. "We'll have to buy it. And what will the price be, since everyone will know we need a jackass? And maybe it would be more complicated than that, than just money." He stared at Costas, Petros, the others. "No. This one is running toward the coast."

Costas, Pavlos, Petros, Giorgos, and the others were gone. Boot sat on the chair and stared at the empty street. The store owner sat on his step and cried, and his wife, a bearded, shrewish woman, shouted and ran every now and then into the store to retrieve a bit of broken mirror, a bent spoon, a dented pail, broken lanterns. She stood before her husband with the bits of trash as though she were exhibiting the tools of a despicable trade. The store owner bobbed his head, looked at her with no shame, with the tears running down his cheeks.

"Do you have a bottle opener?" said Boot.

The store owner pawed at the things his wife had left around his feet.

"I don't know," said the store owner.

"You don't know," said his wife, opening her hand in contempt. "Sure we got an opener."

"One can opener," said Boot.

The woman disappeared.

"She didn't see it," said the store owner. "She didn't fight with the beast."

Boot took the bottle opener from the woman, paid her, and dropped it into his pocket.

Boot bought two bottles of beer from the taverna owner, put them in the bicycle basket, and threw a leg over the cardboard seat. He was pedaling again, although weaving more than the last time because of the bicycle's front wheel: it looked as though it were slowly melting. The beer bottles rattled against each other, made a clear sound in the harsh sunlight and empty streets. Boot stood on the pedals, feeling as dysfunctional as the machine, but pumping anyway. People on the veranda and at the windows of the home for the aged had been only momentarily confused: running fishermen and merchants, the jackass and the girl, Boot riding the bicycle as though straight from the garbage heap of Hades, were accepted as proof of senility.

The merchants and fishermen were no longer enjoying the contest, the chance to race one another. When Boot passed they didn't bother to look at him, since at this point they were only concerned with staying upright, keeping their legs in motion, desperately trying not to give in to the heat and sun, both of which they had respected all their lives, as their fathers had before them, rising early, taking siesta, and finishing the working day in the late afternoon and evening. Those at the rear of the grunting procession struggled most. Their faces were clearly set by the pain of exertion. The jackass slowed to a trot, moved jerkily along the dirt road that led away from the village, along the bluff above the sea, but the seemingly tired, more accessible gait was still charged by terror, as though the jackass weren't resting for itself so much as to give its fear more strength.

Boot pedaled in the sunlight. The jackass ran along the coast, stopped, turned, and watched as Boot approached. Boot stopped, too, and the bicycle struck the stones in the road as it fell. The bottles clinked together as they rolled out, but they didn't break, and Boot was after them, crawling on the hot stones. He opened one bottle and put the other in the bicycle basket. The jackass stared. Boot sat on a large stone that projected over the water, watched the jackass, then took a step forward and stopped: the jackass moved a step farther up the road.

Maybe they should have brought the gun. I'd rather turn in harness myself than catch this jackass.

The fishermen and merchants began arriving, singly, each finding it difficult to stand still after having run so far. Pavlos was the last. He stopped, looked over his shoulder, gauged the distance, and looked pleased that he hadn't dropped dead.

"That's my bike," he said to Boot. "I saw there's something wrong with the wheel."

Pavlos spoke with puffed clusters of words.

"Catch your breath," said Costas.

"No," said Pavlos. "There's something wrong with the wheel."

Boot watched his nodding shadow.

"I'll get another," said Boot.

"Where?" said Pavlos.

"I'll straighten the spokes and the rim," said Boot.

"For the love of God," said Petros.

The jackass seemed to have a finely attenuated sense of distance: Boot raised an arm and the animal moved an arm's length farther up the road.

There were signs every hundred meters or so that had drawings of shells and warnings against touching one.

"How are you going to straighten it?" said Pavlos. "You can't even stand up."

Boot drank some of the cold beer. *It's the north end of the island, the part that was most heavily shelled during the war.*

"Drunk," said Pavlos.

It wasn't exactly a marathon, but a considerable distance had been covered and the shopkeepers and fishermen took the pleasure of cross-country runners. Boot drank the rest of the beer and stared at Pavlos and rolled the bottle in his direction.

"Here," said Boot. "There's a deposit on the bottle."

Boot looked at the reddish soil.

"Go on," he said, pushing the bottle a little closer to Pavlos. "Take it."

The merchants and fishermen watched Pavlos pick the bottle up and put it in his pocket.

"You have no decency," said Pavlos.

"That's true," said Boot. "I drink your liquor."

Petros laughed.

Boot rocked from side to side: his shadow looked like black elastic.

"See," said Pavlos.

"Whatever," said Boot.

Costas and Giorgos stalked the jackass, approached it with winded stealth. The animal moved up the road. Costas and Giorgos thought they could jump the jackass's reflexes, but they were wrong. By the time they had moved, the jackass was already running, the girl already bouncing on its back. The burden appeared resilient, strangely animate. Boot noticed that all the shadows around his were gone, except for one, and when he looked up, he saw Petros.

"I should have taken it in my boat," said Petros.

"No," said Boot. "This is nothing. If you had taken it in your boat there would have been a cyclone."

The last shadow was gone.

My mouth was all cut up when she saw me. From the can.

The sun was so bright that the sky seemed bleached. Boot watched the damaged wheel as it turned over its own shadow. He pumped hard, tried to stay in the center of the road. The bottle of beer bounced in the basket. The jackass had disappeared around a protruding ridge, one that crossed the island like a rib, as though there were a system of internal braces: the island seemed to be the product of a shipyard that used for its materials dirt and stone. Boot heard the insects' neon buzzing. The merchants and fishermen ran in a small group held together by fatigue; they no longer cared about competition or playing, being only concerned that one of them wouldn't ride tandem with the girl. Boot avoided the larger stones. The buzzing of the insects was so loud that the sound seemed to have taken on the physical proportions of a gas.

"When it stops again," said Boot.

"You mean if," said Petros. "*If* it stops again."

"That's what I mean," said Boot.

They came around the ridge and saw that the jackass had run straight out. Boot could see a barely noticeable but moving dot at the end of the road.

He was straining again, off the seat, pumping hard, hearing the bottle bounce in the basket. The bobbing and cardiopathic group was gone, and Boot headed after the animal.

It's hardly ever off the road except at home, and then it turns in the harness.

In each tree there were so many birds that they seemed to be some feathery issue, a squawking growth attached to bark and leaves, trunks and limbs. Even the birds had enough sense to stay out of the heat.

The ruins were still intact: some of the stones seemed as sharp as the day they had been cut from the quarry. The columns were ribbed and grooved, made of white marble, marred here and there by ashy grain, worn smooth by the island's harsh weather. Across the top of each column was a long, narrow section of marble, a remnant of the roof. Inside the outer walls were reddish mounds, time-mired foundations. But it was still possible to make out the size and shape of rooms, the arrangement of houses, the location of paths. The houses were on a slope beneath broad terraces, wide sections of steps. The foundations farthest from the marble columns were dim welts in the earth. The entire structure, erratic columns, steps, terraces, and low walls, was clean, surprisingly so, as though there were a superintendent who came each night with his broom and dustpans and gave the place a good sweeping. The road rose along a knoll and then toward a ridge and ended at the ruins. From the main plaza, a broad, flat affair surrounded by columns, there was a view of the water.

Boot leaned the bike against a wall and listened to the sound of the jackass as it climbed the steps to the main plaza. Boot crawled along one of the slowly shifting foundations like some displaced intruder. The jackass stood at the top of the steps, then walked, its hooves still clattering on stone, toward the center of the ancient city, into the political arena or temple, and stopped next to a wall there, a raised circular opening in the stone terrace.

It can smell the water.

Boot sat behind a column, untied his high-topped hiking shoes, and pulled the laces through the eyes. The jackass seemed vaguely catatonic: it stood in the center of the terrace in bright sunlight with drooping ears, shifting eyes. Boot's shoes flopped around his feet as he walked back to the bicycle.

I wonder how far from the top of the well the water is.

He took off his belt and tied it and the laces together. The ruins were silent: Boot thought he could hear the animal breathing. He drank half of the beer quickly, then poured the rest on the reddish earth, and tied the end of one shoelace to the empty bottle. He took off his shoes, put some small stones in the bottom of the bottle, and walked quietly through the arched entrance of the ruins, feeling his bare feet pad against the worn marble, a sense of civilized ridiculousness, his flesh vulnerable against flooring that was two thousand years old.

"Water," he said to the jackass. "A little cold water from the well."

He spoke slowly. The jackass looked at him with inconclusive eyes. The girl had ridden surprisingly well, was still sitting squarely between the wooden X's of the saddletree. The animal seemed to be waiting for the comforting resolution offered by frenzied running.

"Water," said Boot.

The well was covered with a hinged, circular piece of wood that kept the sons and daughters of day-trippers from climbing inside. Boot tried to ignore the suspicious animal and opened the well: the pool at the bottom seemed as unctuous as a piece of ground and polished glass, a lens that held blue sky, Boot, the bottle dangling from shoelaces and a belt. The jackass's ears surveyed the landscape, stopped at

41

the sounds of merchants and fishermen, men who ran now in fatigued parody of themselves.

The water, blue sky, broke into sensual undulations.

"Water in the well," said Boot.

The jackass opened its mouth as wide as possible, turned its dry tongue in the air, brayed. Boot pulled the bottle from the well. Merchants and fishermen struggled up the steps and collapsed into the least bit of shade.

There was a hill that sloped gently upward and away from the ruins. Two merchants and a fisherman strolled, in a manner that they thought passed for stealth, around the side of the marble terrace. Boot watched them slip over the wall. He sprinkled some water on the grayish, veined stones. *It'll evaporate quickly. The jackass will be able to smell it.*

The girl's hair was touched with bits of weeds and wild oats that grew along the side of the road. She seemed sacrificial in the center of the plaza. Boot spilled more water and moved slowly toward the jackass. *I'm glad I can't see her face. Or won't be able to see the old woman's face if they kill this jackass.* Boot poured more water into his hand and approached the animal, grinned, whispered seductively.

"You've got to be thirsty," said Boot. "You've got to."

The animal smelled the water: hooves clicked on the stone. Boot felt the full, dry, faintly haired lips against his hand. The merchants and fishermen began to move from the shade.

"What are you doing?" said Boot, without looking at any of them. "Stay away."

Boot shook his head. The merchants and fishermen heaved and puffed and walked toward the animal. Boot tried to reach for the halter, but Pavlos had already moved, had already made a stab for it.

The jackass spun once and saw the circle of men and ran

for an opening between the columns. Boot was left with the belt, shoelaces, the bottle, a wet outstretched hand.

"You shouldn't have done that," said Boot.

The animal will have to jump, and that's best. Because at least we could get the girl back if she falls off. And then it will be just the animal. Maybe there's a taverna. A little farther up where the day-trippers stop.

The girl moved like grotesque wings. The animal balked once at the edge of the terrace. *No, no, even if she falls, someone will have to carry her.* The animal jumped, trailing rear hooves gracefully over the marble edge, and disappeared, leaving the terrace quiet and charged. The fishermen and merchants and Boot heard the animal falling into the stiff growth at the side of the ruins. The brush flinched. The jackass seemed to be frightened by the sound of its own movement.

"Well," said Boot to Costas, who stood near the edge, "do we have to carry her?"

Boot saw the animal jumping in the stubborn brush, desperately moving toward a more open space. The girl rode as securely as before.

"What?" said Costas.

The animal broke away from the thickest patch and ran up the gently sloping hill, over bushes and stones, bucking in gullies.

"Christ," said Pavlos, "I almost had it."

Yucca, cactus, soil colored by the island's ferrous deposits, plants that seemed to thrive on the harsh light alone, needing neither water nor dirt, or perhaps dirt only to rest on: the animal ran with shocked strides. It slipped in a narrow gully, its hooves seeming useless on irregular stone.

"You wouldn't carry her," said Boot.

"I don't have to," said Costas. "She's still on the jackass."

Boot made a quick gesture of contempt and watched some of the merchants and fishermen climbing down the sides of the ruins but not walking into the brush, being instinctively afraid, as were all islanders, of walking too far from roads and places where many feet had gone before.

"I'm not walking out there," said Boot to Pavlos.

"You shouldn't have been surly," said Pavlos. "If you hadn't, none of us would have to walk out there."

Boot could feel his eyes.

"You," said Boot, "you walk out there. Look, if you walk out there I'll buy a ticket to America."

"I told you," said Pavlos.

The others, those who had climbed from the ruins, stood before the brush, stared at the animal, picked at their palms. The rest of the men began shuffling toward the edge of the plaza, although none dared look another in the eyes.

Boot walked to a rectangular piece of shade, a shadow of a crossbeam that ran between two columns, and leaned against the base. *Might as well wait. If we're lucky, it won't be long.*

"Throw stones at it," screamed Boot.

The merchants and fishermen stared at him.

"We should have brought a gun," said Petros.

"No," said Boot. "That wouldn't do it."

The merchants and fishermen gathered stones, cradled them in their arms, waited until everyone had enough.

"Keep quiet," said Costas.

The animal stood with splayed legs on a bald patch in the brush. It chewed awkwardly at the dusty shrubs, jerked its head away, then bit again. The girl still rested firmly between the wooden saddletrees, her hair filled with bits of brush in addition to the yellow wild oats: she looked like a child who had been rolling down hillsides. The animal ate in a mild stupor.

It's just got to find the right spot, that's all. And they'll help with the stones.

"I guess it will feel good," said Boot to Costas, who had taken a step or two toward the edge of the marble terrace. Boot stared at the mounds of reddish dirt, the slowly dissolving foundations.

"You don't know what you're talking about," said Costas. "You're stupid and you don't know anything."

Boot chuckled, looked at the brownish hills, the rubbled landscape: all of it had the tone of a lot where a house has just been torn down.

"And you," said Boot, still chuckling quietly in the shade, just feeling the effect of the sun, the dusty tightening of the skin on his face. "You . . ." He shook his head. "A fart has no nose."

Petros threw the first stone, but it landed a long way from the mark. The jackass turned an ear toward the sound of the stone striking brush.

"Shit," said Boot.

"Could you do better?" said Pavlos.

"Get lost," said Boot. He walked to the well, stepped into his shoes, laced them up, and put on his belt.

Boot shook his head, watched the men throw stones. *Now it isn't just garbage and a bike, plates, knives, buckets, and wire that's chasing it, but the island itself.*

The jackass was struck squarely in the middle of the forehead. Boot stared, amazed and angry that the fisherman could have the vanity to take pleasure in accuracy, in having hit the animal in the head. The jackass was momentarily stunned. Boot sat in the shade, no longer chuckling: he just watched, being now bereft even of contempt.

The animal spun and was struck again, wheeled and started, being more afraid, it seemed, of stones that fell around it than those that didn't, more afraid of the sound, of possibility, than fact.

So it stood in the center of the bald spot, trapped there, listening to the rustling brush, flinching as each stone fell.

"There's something you haven't thought of," said Boot.

Costas looked at him with an expression as blank as a tombstone.

"It can't be helped," said Costas.

They're going to hit the girl.

It sounded like someone beating a rug: the animal was struck on the leg, head, side. Boot leaned against the column, and watched. The merchants and fishermen labored in the heat and light. The air was filled with reddish dust, and Boot could smell it as he sat against the column running one finger down a groove in the stone. The animal ran into a weathered crevice, where it stumbled and rolled, kicking four hooves into the air and revealing, for a moment, a heaving belly. Boot felt as though he were dissolving, as though his flesh were spreading over the terrace: he tapped his head gently against the reassuring stone. The jackass rocked back and forth and then found its footing and jumped back into the brush. The girl was still held against the saddle, but the saddle was canted to one side. Her head struck the rocks in the gully.

The men looked for more stones, picked them up and threw them in one motion, not actually watching the animal but listening and throwing stones into the brush where the animal kicked at the misunderstood torment. Boot saw the blood in sharp contrast against the grayish fur, the hairless nose as the animal jumped a gully and ran toward the ruins, being now so disoriented it lacked even the idea of where the stones were coming from. But soon the animal had a very good idea: it was struck more times than Boot could count, on the forehead, lips, neck, legs. The jackass tried to slide, putting its feet forward and squatting so deeply that its ass touched the ground, then turned and exposed the girl, her nude legs and buttocks. Her skin was scratched, but she didn't bleed. The sight of the girl didn't stop the merchants and fishermen. Perhaps it even intensified their efforts, since they were so sharply confronted with the object of their failure. They continued throwing stones, striking the girl as well.

So now it is the animal alone who will protect her.

Costas saw Boot staring at him.

"It won't take long," said Costas.

"What you need is a metal detector," said Boot.

"What you need is to keep your mouth shut," said Costas.

If they had a metal detector, they could comb the hill and find it and run the jackass across it and be done.

The animal ran from the ruins, after having been close enough to the line of men for one of them to have grabbed the halter or even the girl, but the merchants and fishermen did neither, didn't grab the rope because they were too intent on finding and throwing stones, didn't grab the girl because they were afraid to touch what they had sought for so long.

The animal ran again, pushing through brush, jumping gullies, getting far enough away from the men so that the stones fell behind it more often than they fell in front. The girl now was dragged at the animal's side, her arms and head scraping against rocks and brush: she looked like a stuntman from an early Hollywood movie. And then the jackass was completely out of range, running near the top of the ridge, but the merchants and fishermen continued to throw stones, realizing that otherwise they would simply have to stand and watch, being unable to inflict an outrageous and painful necessity on a jackass and a dead girl.

Their frustration was stronger than ever, since they had luxuriated in anger and were now trapped by it, exposed. None could look at another or at Boot.

It isn't doing me any favor at all.

Boot pushed his back and head against the column.

The air trembled. The merchants and fishermen peered from the brush next to the ruins as bits of dirt settled around them, fell into the stubborn growth. There was a shred of flesh on one of the columns, a bit of hide on the marble, unidentifiable parts on one side of the crater, a jagged hole where Boot had last seen the jackass and the girl. They were separated now. But the jackass, even at the last, had protected the girl, had borne the greatest part of the explosion and was itself shorn almost completely in half: it looked as though some large beast had taken a bite from the animal's midsection, leaving only a shred of hide to hold front and hindquarters together.

The flesh doesn't forget. A hind leg kicked and quivered. *Not if it's run that much.*

The girl lay in the brush, the side of her face pushed against a thick branch, her legs and arms torn but not bleeding, seeming strangely inanimate after the continuous jerking of the animal's gait. Boot had begun to believe that she was alive, having absorbed some of the animal's vitality and terror. But now he looked at her with the same horrified disbelief as when he first saw her.

"It ran across a shell," said Costas.

Boot laughed.

"It couldn't be helped," said Costas.

"Fuck you," said Boot in English.

"What?" said Costas.

I've got to remember where the jackass walked.

"Well?" said Boot.

The merchants and fishermen at the edge of the ruins didn't look at Boot or answer: they simply stared at half an animal, the crater, the girl.

"All right," said Boot. "Do you mind if I touch her now?"

The men stared at the crater.

"For the love of God," said Petros.

"Will you?" said Boot to Costas.

Costas sat in the shade and stared at the hill.

"I'll bring my boat," said Petros.

"How are you going to get your boat on that hill?" said Boot.

Petros sat in the shade, too.

"All right," Boot muttered to himself as he unbuttoned his shirt. "Leave the bicycle."

He took off his shirt and climbed down the side of the ruins into the brush. *If it's all right for the jackass, it's all right for me. But at least the animal was more at home on this island than I'll ever be. I'm a stranger to them all, especially because I understand their dignity comes only from its issue: a dead, outraged girl.*

The men watched sullenly from the edge of the ruins. Boot picked his way through the field, always trying to step in the prints made by the jackass's hooves, avoiding the long, irregular marks that ran next to them. Boot glanced up once and saw the temple, the marble columns in relief against the sea cut into silver scales by wind and sunlight.

Petros and Costas toyed with their strings of beads, and the sound echoed in the plaza. Boot approached the crater with some hesitation. *If there had been a second shell, the explosion from the first would have set it off, too. I guess. Or maybe the only way to do it is to run around on all fours and have some men throw stones.*

Boot wrapped his shirt around the girl's head and covered her with the burlap again, feeling it stick in the bush where the girl rested. Some of the men still held stones, and one or two of them looked as though they were still thinking of throwing them, for the same reason, it seemed, that the animal's legs twitched: after having come so far, it was simply hard to stop.

Pavlos was looking at the wheel of his bike.

"Hold it up," said Boot.

Boot stepped over the cardboard seat and rested the girl, face down, on the handlebars and basket.

"I'll bring the bike back," said Boot. "Don't worry about that. And I'll fix the wheel, too."

Pavlos gazed at a shred of hide, rooted by fat to a smooth piece of marble.

"Let go," said Boot.

Pavlos held on to the bike and stared at Boot and said, "Maybe I'll get a new one. My son's been looking in the catalog."

"No," said Boot. "It's got to be fixed. Maybe the boy will want it because of this afternoon alone. Let go."

Pavlos let go. His face was set in an expression of two-cent bitterness.

The men could hear a sound that seemed to come from an express truck loaded with broken beer bottles and scrap metal. There was a trail of dust, too, and it looked like some horizontal tornado that had at the base of its funnel a Renault station wagon. The car came up the road, made the turn, and stopped at the ruins. Thymos left the engine running and got out, looked at Boot and the girl and the bicycle, the shopkeepers, the fishermen, the dead jackass and the crater, and got back into the Renault. He drove toward the village. Boot didn't even bother to shout, since he knew that Thymos wouldn't consider lending his car: no one knew for sure whether the girl had been infected, and Thymos sold food.

"At least he'll tell Ulla," said Boot. "That will save me something."

Boot rode away from the ruins, glancing over his shoulder once to see Costas, Pavlos, Giorgos, the fishermen and merchants, gathering for the long walk back to town, during which there would be time enough for recrimination and silence, the latter being worse because it would reveal the inescapable necessity of their behavior: old hostility, old habits hoarded against deprivation; none would mention any surprise.

Boot struggled with the ruts, then rode slowly in the fluid sense of balance made possible by the paved section of the road, and when he approached the first buildings of the village he kept the bicycle on a line that was equidistant between them: he felt as though he were driving a small airplane.

A villager said, "Where's the jackass?"

Boot stared at the girl's ankles, noticed that they were still tied together. Her skin seemed a little feverish because of the heat. Boot's hands buzzed with alcohol. He had been drunk often enough to know it was going to happen, but he still wondered for a moment if the sensation weren't some lingering vibration in the steel of the bicycle from the explosion.

If it's not with me, not with the girl, he knows it's in pretty bad shape.

Siesta broke. Over his shoulder Boot saw the villagers emerging from doorways, following him as though they were the wake of exhaust, filling the street completely, the men dressed in white shirts, black pants, and wearing dark glasses, the women in black from head to toe, the children in their blue school uniforms. Boot tried to ignore them, as though there were nothing on the handlebars and basket, or that it were already what it would soon become, earth itself, no more outrageous than any field.

After turning from an alley onto the waterfront again and pedaling by the stone wall covered with yellowish nets, the sharp recesses where confined water lapped irregularly, Boot passed the hotel; there was no other way to get to the church, or only one other way, which was too long and circuitous to consider, so it had to be by the hotel, where a small red car was parked, and where Boot could see standing on a terrace, two stories up from the street, a woman in a bathing suit, her hair moving about her shoulders in the mild afternoon breeze. She stared at the girl, the bicycle, and Boot, who looked up once and began to tremble, outraged that it should happen at all, and especially at this time, after months of the most vicious indifference, which he now realized had been cultivated because he had mistaken it for strength.

Boot heard the old people in their home. Three or four were even singing the same song, but they didn't sing it together. Others hummed and chanted, vented whatever surfaced in leathery minds, the number of children born, articles in a dowry, stones removed from a single, barren piece of land, children lost. On the veranda Boot saw the continually startled, confused, cataracted faces: they stared at the bits of garbage, the girl delicately balanced across the handlebars, the street clotted with silent people.

The priest, who wore immaculate robes, a full beard, and who had his hair pulled into a bun, said, "In here."

Boot stood in the incense-filled room, felt the dull weight in his arms (the girl weighed less than a hundred pounds), and stared at the priest.

"In here," said the priest.

Boot left the girl on a table in the center of the room, took his shirt from her head, and put it on. He turned away from the priest and stood with the bicycle. The villagers had assembled in the intersection before the gates of the church, about thirty feet away: none dared come any closer. Boot looked at them and saw at the side of the street, gently and unobtrusively pushing toward the front of the villagers, the woman from the hotel, who was now dressed in blue pants, a red shirt, and sandals, and who gazed at Boot with something more than curiosity. The villagers began to drift away, but the woman continued staring: Boot had a deep tan, sandy hair, green eyes, was a man in remarkably good shape for a drunk, trim and agile, a man who stood in the bright sunlight with his chin and lips covered with blood, his cheek bruised, one eye swollen almost shut. Then even the children were leaving, their blue uniforms revolving slowly past the white plaster walls. The woman turned, hesitated, and then walked in the direction of the hotel.

She could have given me a lift.

But Boot wouldn't have known what to say to Ulla about the car: she had been in an automobile only once before, on the day Boot borrowed one to bring his things from the village to the house where he now lived. He had left the car in the opium smuggler's yard and carried his clothes, books, plates, and liquor over the ridge and into the valley, and when he was walking back toward the opium smuggler's yard, Ulla had stopped him and said, I'm going to town. Will you take me. And Boot said, Yes. And when Ulla saw the car, a jeep, she said, Will you wait, and Boot said, Yes, and Ulla squatted behind a rock and lifted her skirts: she was afraid that she'd urinate on the seats. So they drove along the sea. Ulla was terrified of the movement and the noise, but they listened to the Turkish songs of lament on the radio, and that comforted her some, because at least she had heard a radio before. And now, if she saw the car or heard that Boot had come in one, that it was parked in the opium smuggler's yard, she'd look at Boot and say, How am I going to get it into harness.

Maybe I should have brought a piece of hide. At least then she'd know I hadn't sold her jackass.

Boot rode the bicycle down to the waterfront, to Pavlos' taverna, and the boy gave him beer and ouzo.

"I'll need the bike for a while," said Boot.

Pavlos, Costas, Giorgos, the other fishermen, farmers, and merchants, drifted into the taverna separately, obviously having found it difficult to walk with those whom they had raced before. But they still came to the taverna, hoping that it, at least, had remained unsullied, that it still offered a sense of luxury. Each walked in, looked at Boot, and took a seat as far away from him as possible, and then each one of them got quietly drunk, except for Pavlos, who had only one drink and said to his son, "We'll get a new bike."

Boot waited for the last one. He listened to the sound of the water against the stone quay.

Boot said, "No one brought the saddle."

"What?" said Petros.

"Not one of you," said Boot, pouring ouzo into his glass, "brought back the saddle. Or the halter and rope."

Boot waited and drank. Through a window of the taverna he could see the night sealed at the horizon.

"You've had too much to drink," said Pavlos.

Pavlos turned on two electric bulbs that filled the room with a greasy, golden light: it colored and softened the furniture, chairs of matting and unfinished wood, tables with tops worn so thin they were almost translucent. Boot ate slowly, having to think about the most basic motions. He ate a meal of bread, olives, oil, and an onion. He dipped the bread into the oil. The oil was golden, the same color as the light that came from the bulbs.

"I'll need the bike," said Boot.

"You walked to town," said Pavlos. "You can walk home."

"I'll take you home," said Petros, "in my boat."

Boot cleaned his plate with a piece of bread. The men watched him, each one knowing he should have thought a little more clearly, or simply done what heritage demanded. They felt more insulted than ever that a stranger, a foreigner, would do for them what they should have done themselves.

"I'm not going home," said Boot.

"Where are you going?" said Pavlos.

"Christ," said Boot. "How much?"

"For the food?" said Pavlos.

The men looked unctuous and jaundiced in the light from the two bulbs.

"No," said Boot. "For a jackass."

"Depends on the age," said Costas.

"How old was this one?" said Boot.

"Four," said Pavlos.

"Four, then," said Boot. "How much is it for one that's four? Maybe even three. For aggravation."

"Fifteen hundred," said Pavlos.

"You're crazy," said a fisherman. "Theodore's, the one that took the races last year, that made three hundred in bets alone, only went for a thousand."

Fifteen hundred, a fifty-dollar bill.

"You don't understand," said Boot. "Everyone knows we need one."

"We?" said Costas. "What's this 'we'? You borrowed it."

The islanders realized it had been a mistake to sit so far away from Boot, since his chair was next to the door.

Boot began to grin.

"And what did you do?" said Boot.

Costas looked at his shoes.

"There were ten of us," said Boot. "That makes it easy."

A fisherman glanced at the door.

"So it's only a hundred and fifty apiece," said Boot. "Although I really shouldn't pay anything at all, seeing as how I only borrowed it, leaving you to do the killing."

The men sat in the taverna's jaundiced light and stared at Boot and realized suddenly that they were drawn to the responsibility, a hideous one because it left them no choice in the matter. They knew, too, that they couldn't beat Boot and throw him into the harbor, since that would only make matters worse. Two or three of the men considered it for a moment, but rejected it when they realized that everyone on the island would know why the beating had taken place, would know that the men in the taverna had violated the islanders' basic ethic: acceptance of burdens already yoked to shoulders.

"Give," said Boot. "One-fifty apiece."

"You should be careful," said Petros.

Petros put a hundred and fifty on the table in front of Boot and walked out the door.

Costas put money on the table.

The shopkeepers, those dressed in white shirts and black pants, and the fishermen, in white denim, walked by the table one at a time and left the correct amount, usually in wrinkled and soiled bills.

There were two who didn't have money, and for those Boot took a hundred and fifty from the taverna's till. They signed IOUs. Boot took Pavlos' share from the till also. As the men passed Boot, each glanced at him with the same blank and thoughtless hostility that the island presented to those who see it from a ship for the first time, the same that farmers turned toward the fields each morning, forcing on the land what it forced on them.

After the last man had left, Boot took a bill from the table and stuck it into the till. Pavlos sat on one of his chairs and stared at Boot with the same thoughtless hostility. Boot took a bottle of ouzo from the shelf above the icebox.

"That money's supposed to go for the animal," said Pavlos.

Boot shook his head.

"A jackass will never cost fifteen hundred," said Boot. "Not when I buy it, when word gets around where I got the money." Boot stared at the bottle, started, and said, "Goddamn."

"What?" said Pavlos.

Because they'll tell it as though it had been their idea, that they themselves realized the necessity of buying their way out of this taverna. And shame everyone who has a jackass to sell (and that's not many) into yielding to that same sense of necessity that required each of them to leave a hundred and fifty on the table. And Gold help the man who refuses to be shamed.

Boot scooped up the bills on the table and stared through

the panes of the front door, the framed squares of distorting glass through which he could see only points of light from the masts of ships torn into crosses, the smeared and pear-shaped globes that were strung along the waterfront.

"You're going to make a mistake," said Pavlos.

Boot said, "I already have."

Boot drank from the bottle and replaced the cork.

"Maybe they'll take some of it back," said Boot.

"Not a chance," said Pavlos. "Not one of them, not even you, want to be reminded of how that money was taken in the first place."

Boot nodded, stared at the blank hostility, the shopkeeper's shrug of acquiescence.

"You should be scared shitless," said Pavlos.

I am.

Pavlos sat alone in the yellow light. Boot dropped the bottle into the bicycle basket and pedaled through the empty streets, cut here and there by light from doors and windows. At the corner of the road that ran along the coast he saw a lighted, ragged opening, heard loud voices and weeping, and recognized the shop that had been invaded by the jackass. The shopkeeper and his wife were trying to put their wares in order, shifting through a slowly diminishing pile of broken jars, plates, bent spoons, blankets, overturned sacks of flour, dented cans of precious imported foodstuffs. Boot noticed the shadow of the bicycle on the cobblestones: the machine seemed, in distortion, both complicated and monstrous. He leaned it against a whitewashed wall.

"I need a lantern," said Boot.

The shopkeeper started, but then looked again at his goods with a hatred that had been cultivated over a lifetime. Boot stood in the door, pleased that the array of objects so perfectly meshed with his state of mind. The shopkeeper's wife sorted the wares. Boot joined her and found what he wanted: a pump kerosene lantern, a wick, and, at the back of the shop, a jug of kerosene to fill the lantern's belly. The shopkeeper kicked a bucket and hissed.

"It's dead," said the wife.

"Too bad," said the shopkeeper. "There are things I would like to have done."

The new wick burned to the consistency of the most delicate ash of the finest lace, its delicacy alone seeming special in such a place as the island, as though the ash were the ghost of infinite luxury, a piece of lace found in the remains of an elaborate cremation, lace handed from mother to daughter for generations, and finally consumed in the pyre of one who had lost even more than life: a woman without a child to receive an honored possession.

Boot pumped the lantern until its light was as white as the stars beyond the harbor. He hung it on the bicycle and left a note for a hundred on a nail that stuck out of the door.

If they were willing to pay for the jackass, at least willing to be reminded what it takes to live on this island, then they should be willing to contribute a little something to this shop. Because they beat the trash-can lids together. And, anyway, it cuts down the profit. The goddamn profit.

But the island was beautiful, and beguiling, too: houses that looked as though they had been cut from blocks of white plaster, fronted with arbors of green vines and ripe grapes. There were a few golden fields, steep and small, and sandy beaches, the clearest of all water, the seemingly effortless ease with which people went about their business. The pace was slow but insidious. A newcomer would feel only the most mild release after arriving, but as the weeks passed the difficulty of getting anything done made itself apparent, and once apparent, claustrophobic, so that the beauty of the place became tainted.

Boot stood in front of the shop.

"I told you," said the woman to her husband. The shop-keeper held the pieces of a Styrofoam ice chest, pushed them together as though the cooler were some three-dimensional jigsaw puzzle, one that required more than just patience. "I told you a jackass would never cost fifteen hundred. Look."

She took the note from the nail and held it under her husband's nose. The shopkeeper dropped the chest and turned to a plastic tub filled with debris and began muttering to himself, beyond caring or calculation. His wife took no notice of the fact, not even when the shopkeeper hissed again. She was concerned only about the price of the jackass and the correctness of her estimation. She smiled at Boot and nodded and said, "He's confused."

Boot stepped into the circle of light broken only by the frame of the bicycle and then by his pumping legs as he rode in the same direction as earlier, but this time not so fast, listening to the hum of the cooling land, the rustle of the rough shrubs, water hissing around the rocks below the road.

No, there's no need to hurry, because what's left of the animal is still in the middle of the field, where there could be other shells, although I doubt it, since the animal looked so hard to find that one. But people probably think there are more, and if they went to butcher the animal, to get a little meat for stew, a bit of hide to use as a hinge, they'd be afraid. And, in any case, they wouldn't butcher the animal because they'd be afraid of the shrapnel, of eating it. So the animal will be there and the pack saddle, too, because no one would walk into the field to get the saddle if he couldn't get a little meat as well.

I want to see the small blue veins behind her knees.

He rode the rest of the way to the ruins, finding a joy in riding a bicycle he hadn't felt since childhood. The darkness of the island's night was startling, vacuous. Boot left the bicycle at the steps of the ruins, took the lantern and climbed to the ancient plaza, and saw the skeletal marble. Then he was on the other side of the plaza and in the brush, pushing through it, able to make out the tracks of men and those of the animal, his own footprints, and finally the kinetic shadow of the crater's edge. The animal still lay in the same position, but now it seemed more mutilated than before, as though the time spent lying in the dirt and brush had been as damaging as the explosion itself. Boot reached into the cold opening to uncinch the saddle. The alcohol had made the tips of his fingers numb and he was pleased that he couldn't feel the texture of frigid organs, tripe, torn hide. The slight tickling began on the backs of his hands and spread to his arms, and Boot realized that the ants from the wound, if you can call the place where a body has been roughly sheared a wound, were moving over what seemed to be warmer and fresher remains, his own flesh. The animal's head was thrown backward and distorted by the shadows, and Boot saw the black lines streaming away from its eyes. The cinch was torn and sticky. Boot pulled the saddle and what was left of the cinch from the animal's back and left them next to the hindquarters.

I'll have to get a new one, a new cinch, but they aren't very expensive, and, anyway, a new one will help soothe Ulla.

Boot supported himself for a moment with a leg that was as stiff as a cane: he held it by the hoof. The tickling continued. Light from the lantern revealed ants on the pack saddle, too, tentatively picking their way through the thickening spots of blood. Boot scrubbed the saddle with handfuls of dirt from the crater's edge, felt the soil scratch the wooden frame. Beyond the circle of light there was the abrasive sound of insects. Boot took the halter and lifted the animal's head so he could get to the buckle on the other side, disturbing momentarily the ant's path. The halter was sticky and cold, too, and Boot took it to the edge of the crater and scrubbed it with dirt, and then, when the tickling had reached his upper arms and back, took off his shirt and snapped it in the dry air. The animal seemed more violated than ever, since even the process of decay had been interrupted. Boot carried the saddle and halter to the plaza, where he stopped and slapped at his back and neck and chest.

The beer bottle was still next to the wall. There was water inside, and Boot poured it over his hands and rubbed them together and wiped them on his pants. He sat on the steps next to the saddle and halter and then went for the bottle of ouzo and sat again drinking in the slowly diminishing light of the lantern. Every now and then he worked the pump, increased the pressure so that the light shone more brightly over worn marble, ribbed columns, the foundations of ancient houses that now had the aspect of burial mounds. Boot felt reassured by used stone, old marble, objects that had borne witness to any number of nights such as this one, any number of indignities, insults, murders, intrigues, the marble itself being subjected only to the island's harsh weather, something that had, without doubt, contributed to centuries of brutality.

Boot walked across the plaza to the bicycle, where he put the halter and the bottle in the basket and with his shoelaces tied the saddle to the small platform behind the seat. He began pedaling back to town, pleased by the evening breeze, the effect of the alcohol, the hissing lantern. He was still aware of the tickling of the ants.

He rode until he came to the second light. There was a lantern hung on a hook in the wooden frame covered with grapevines. The frame had been built over a front porch. A farmer and his wife sat in chairs, their faces and bodies marked by the shadows of the eddy of moths moving about the glass bell of the lantern. Boot leaned the bicycle against the stone wall of the porch. The farmer and his wife stared at the dead horizon, seeing, every now and then, the lights that marked the slow passage of a ship.

Boot stepped into the light. The farmer and his wife stared through the moving shadows of the insects.

"I need to buy a jackass," said Boot.

The old man looked away from the darkness beyond the porch and stared at Boot.

"I borrowed it," said Boot. "She's turning in harness now. You know her."

"Yes," said the farmer.

The farmer looked at the bills stuffed haphazardly into Boot's shirt pocket.

"You shouldn't carry money that way," said the farmer.

Boot took the bills from his pocket and folded them neatly. He stumbled on the first step, fell partway up the stairs, and said, "I'm sorry. It's dark here. How much is the jackass?"

"Not so dark as you're drunk," said the woman.

"Quiet," said the farmer.

"How much?" said Boot.

The woman hissed something that Boot couldn't hear.

"Don't talk," said the farmer. "It's five hundred."

"No," said Boot. *If I needed proof, that's it. Five hundred is so low that something's got to be cooking, because no one on the island gives up that much without the guarantee of payment, if not in cash, then in the coin of things I'd rather not think about.*

"No," said Boot.

The farmer looked as though his guts were made out of beer bottles and someone had given him a good kick: it was the first time he'd seen a low price refused.

"It's a good price," said the woman.

"Not enough," said Boot.

"You'd be surprised," said the farmer. He stared at the horizon.

"I'm sure I would," said Boot.

The bunches of grapes seemed waxy, more like purple and fertile sacs for insects than fruit.

"Seven-fifty," said the woman.

"Quiet," said the farmer.

"No," said Boot.

He walked down the steps to the circle of light, the bicycle.

The old man said, "Opium smuggler . . ."

Boot mounted the bicycle and began to pedal; the desolation of the road gave the night a medieval quality. The food had lessened the effect of the alcohol, but Boot was still sloppy: the bicycle slipped in a rut and collapsed, and Boot swore and felt the tickling again, but this time he knew it wasn't the ants so much as food for them, a line of blood that ran down the lower part of his arm from his elbow.

The windows of the houses in the village were open, and it wasn't just the heat (the houses at the end of the day were as hot as clay ovens), since most people kept their windows closed night and day, hoping that jerry-built seals would keep out the dust and heat: it was because the houses lined the path Boot would most likely take back from the ruins, either walking and leading a jackass (burdened with a bicycle and bought at a price so far below market value as to make Boot visibly tremble in his shoes), or simply riding the bicycle, looking for another place to buy an animal.

The quay was stripped of nets: the fishermen had them in the small bays around the island. The quay was lighted by a string of bulbs, each about a hundred feet from the next, and they gave the harbor a forbidding aspect: it was deserted in the same way that fairs are at night, being not just without people, but stark because so many had been there recently. Boot stopped at the central square, named for an ancient mathematician who had been born on the island, and drank at the fountain. On the terrace of the best room in the hotel the woman sat in a chair and leaned her elbows on the railing.

Boot pedaled to the end of the waterfront, turned the corner, got off the bicycle, and waited. A villager sat in the open window above Boot's head. The bicycle leaned against a wall marked by bullets: it looked as though it had been standing there since the end (and the duration, too) of the war. Boot rocked back and forth on his heels, waited, looked around the corner, and saw that the woman was gone. The quay was filled with the sound of water confined by stone.

It wasn't the heat that drove her to the terrace.

Boot had a drink of ouzo and rode past the pocked houses and was glad when he came to the outskirts of the village. The paved section of road ended abruptly and the bicycle moved sideways on the gravel. The road was nothing more than a flat space gouged in the side of the island by a bulldozer, open earth that had quickly become gullied, creased by weather. Boot grinned and worked the bicycle: he had reached that state of drunkenness where obvious danger is pleasant.

No one would come to such a place as this without the desire (or the belief in the desire) to be alone: and this one finds herself sitting up half the night to catch a glimpse of a lunatic on a bicycle. Because, maybe, if it happened to her, too, she'd have to attach herself to the first thing she saw. And then she ran across a dead girl on a jackass.

Boot stood over the fallen bicycle, grabbed the lantern by its glass bell, burned his hand.

"Where's the fucking bottle?"

He held the lantern by its wire handle and searched the gullies, kicked stones out of the way, raked the weeds at the side of the road with his fingers, found a horned toad and threw it into the sea. There had been no sound of breaking glass. Boot continued to look in the gullies and weeds, swearing and grabbing for each slick point, whether on a stalk of wild oats or in the mica of a stone. The bicycle lay in the road. Boot kicked it and became angrier still: the bottle lay beneath the basket.

He followed the ruts more carefully. There were olive trees on the upper side of the road, a precipice on the other, the sea hissing around stones. Boot no longer wanted to think about necessity or anything. He drank slowly, wanting to save some because the opium smuggler might not give him a bottle for the trip back to town, but nevertheless hoping the opium smuggler would, in which case Boot could drink what he had left and the new bottle, too.

There was a light in the monastery, and Lukas was standing in the road, watching the lantern on Boot's bicycle weave and bounce in the darkness, appearing as insubstantial as a firefly. Boot pedaled and saw the light and then the monk. *At least there's another who's not afraid. Or one who's lived with fear so long that it seems like a natural element.*

"It's past your bedtime," said Boot. "There's no need to stand in the road all night."

The monk's face was invisible: the interior of the habit seemed to feed on darkness.

"I was only going to wait once," said Lukas.

"I've been warned," said Boot.

"Then there's no need to stand around in the road," said Lukas. "I was only going to do it once."

"Go to bed," said Boot, waving a hand into the darkness beyond the lantern.

Boot pedaled away from the monk, now finding the road more difficult, since this part, between the monastery and the opium smuggler's yard, was less traveled and meant to be so. There wasn't even the gentle path within the road, the effect of countless steps of daily foot traffic.

I really should have sent a message by Petros to the village and hid in the house and waited for someone with less superstition and a boat or for someone with respect and a jackass. Or maybe courage and a car, courage because the car would have to be parked in the opium smuggler's yard. But warnings aren't any good, not after the woman.

The opium smuggler's yard was quiet. Boot leaned the bicycle against a tree, took the lantern from the handlebars, and walked toward one of the low buildings made from the island's stone.

No dog. He always keeps a dog with him so he can tell if someone's coming. He's someplace with the dog, so that means he probably doesn't want anyone around.

Boot could see two other buildings on the slope below the yard.

I need it. Tonight.

He walked through the yard, stopped at the bicycle, and picked up the bottle. Small puffs of dust, looking as though they'd just been released from an aerosol can, rose around his feet as he walked. The insects began to gather around the bell of the lantern. *Something about all the blood or juice or living slime moving to one side of the moth's body, toward warmth and light, so that the insect is drawn by the ballast of its own guts to the flame.*

The dog barked in the farthest hut, one that was built next to a switchback that led down the face of the precipice to the opium smuggler's private dock. Boot walked toward the sound, touching his pocket once, with the hand that held the bottle, to see if the money was still there, not being concerned now whether it was folded, since as far as the opium smuggler was concerned, Boot could have carried cash around in a shopping bag or a bucket.

"Hey," said Boot. "Hey, shhhhh."

The dog barked at his heels, having jumped quickly from the door, from the light that cut the yard. But then it was dark again, and Boot and the dog confronted each other: the threat seemed multiplied, simply because the dog filled so much unseen space with noise and movement.

"Shhh," said Boot again. He kicked the animal. The barking changed to a whimpering and there was the rush of lively movement, a wagging tail, tentative sniffs.

"That's better," said Boot.

The cold nose felt good against the back of Boot's sunburned hands. He stopped for a moment to pet the dog, bunching one ear together, stroking the dusty fur of the dog's neck.

"Shit," said Boot.

He opened the door from which the dog had jumped and saw the opium smuggler pulling away from a cot on which there was a girl. She was fourteen perhaps, naked, her legs spread in an obscene and listless fashion. The hut had a low ceiling and it was hot inside. The girl's pubescent breasts were slick, bright with mixed perspiration, the bones of her hips prominent, not completely covered by the flesh of a woman's body. Boot held the bottle and the lantern. The girl's stomach was flat, untried, touched by a taut navel. She gave off a crystalline odor, one that pierced the stench of the opium smuggler's habits, the closeness of the hut, the smell of burned kerosene. The opium smuggler swore. The girl moved her eyes once toward Boot and pulled her legs together and turned toward the wall. The dog came into the room, walked directly to the cot, and began to sniff. The girl reached over the cot's edge and petted the animal, touched its nose.

The opium smuggler pushed Boot outside and said, "You must be crazy."

"I need a jackass," said Boot.

"Jackass!" screamed the opium smuggler.

Boot nodded.

"And a bottle," said Boot. "I've got money."

He pulled the wad of bills from his shirt and held the bright notes next to the lantern, the gray and moving insects. The opium smuggler grunted. Boot knew that the amount had been calculated to within half a dollar.

"I should have known," said the opium smuggler, "that you'd show up here. But I don't get that every day." A thumb shot from the opium smuggler's fist. Boot glanced at the stone hut.

"I'm in a hurry," said Boot.

The opium smuggler took the bottle and drank. Boot stared at the bobbing larynx.

"They gave you too much money," said the opium smuggler. "That's the problem, isn't it?"

Boot shook his head. The opium smuggler drank again, looked at Boot's outstretched hand, the money, and laughed.

"No," said Boot. "Not gave. Took. I took too much."

The opium smuggler laughed again and squatted in the yard.

"Go on," said Boot, "take it. Times are hard."

The dog barked and the opium smuggler cocked an ear toward the road, waited, and said in a tone that was meant for the animal, "Quiet."

"No bargaining," said Boot. "Fifteen hundred. One bottle and one jackass."

The bills were spread on the ground in front of the opium smuggler.

"Take it," said Boot.

The opium smuggler raked the notes together, gathered paper and dust into his large hand, and stuffed the bills into Boot's pocket.

"I'm glad I'm not in your shoes," said the opium smuggler.

"I don't want to beg," said Boot.

Boot felt on his hand the gentle, fluttering bump of insects as they moved around the lantern's bell.

The opium smuggler laughed. Boot squatted next to him, held the lantern so he could see the opium smuggler's eyes. The opium smuggler shook his head.

"They don't like to be humiliated," said the opium smuggler.

"I need a jackass," said Boot, "and I need a bottle."

The opium smuggler shook his head.

"I guess I was wrong," said Boot, "about you."

The opium smuggler avoided Boot's eyes.

He lives here, too. Goddamn. And smuggles opium and stops roads and seduces fourteen-year-old girls, but that's done almost by license, by the islanders' need for evil, kept at a distance, but evil nevertheless. It's almost as though he were permitted his trespasses to protect fishermen and farmers, so they don't have to worry about themselves: they can point a finger and say, It's there. Out where the road ends. But things are different now. Maybe that farmer or shopkeeper is having a little more trouble pointing that finger. So it wouldn't be stopping a road or anything like it.

The opium smuggler looked at Boot and said, "You're going to have to steal it."

"That's what I was going to do," said Boot. "But I was going to stick the money on a nail."

The opium smuggler said, "Keep the money."

Boot dug at the dirt and the dusty bills in his pocket.

"No," said the opium smuggler. "I don't want it. Anyway, you'll need it for the woman at the hotel."

Boot watched the opium smuggler's eyes, the blank open stare, eyes that had been perfected by generations for dealing with large amounts of cash (which is different from money), men swaying against hysteria, death as commodity.

"I need a bottle," said Boot.

"Sure you do," said the opium smuggler. "It's in the house. The jackass is on a line up the hill."

Boot gathered the bills from the ground and stuck them into the pocket with the others.

The opium smuggler said, "So they'll know that I contributed fifteen hundred myself, as much as all of them put together."

"What?" said Boot, straining in alcoholic disbelief.

71

"Don't you think that's a better idea?" said the opium smuggler.

"What?" said Boot. "That I can't even steal it?"

The opium smuggler nodded and smiled and said, "The animal's yours. As a gift. And I can think of it as insurance."

The opium smuggler chuckled.

"I made a mistake," said Boot.

He sat in the dust and drank.

"There aren't any mistakes," said the opium smuggler. "That's the beauty of it."

So Boot thought of opium and said, "Maybe there's something you want."

The opium smuggler shrugged.

Shit. So that's it. I'm surprised he didn't shoot the girl and put her on the beach himself, knowing that I'd find her. Or have the woman in the hotel shipped in, too.

"I guess there is something," said Boot.

The opium smuggler grunted again.

"I'll need two things," said Boot. "I'll need a little time, and I'll need you to keep your mouth shut. About the animal."

"I'll keep quiet," said the opium smuggler. "For a while."

The empty bottle rolled in the dust.

"I'm going inside," said the opium smuggler. "You've got a little time. If you can't do something with it, don't come around anymore."

The opium smuggler was inside. Boot felt the gentle bump and flutter of insects and listened for telltale sounds from the hut, the creak of a cot, a voice, but he heard nothing. *The son of a bitch. He was just waiting.* Boot shook the dirt out of his pocket. In the largest hut, the opium smuggler's house, Boot smelled the odor that exists where a man

72

lives alone and without running water: acrid and damp, bitter. The air itself seemed to be greasy. Boot overturned a chair, a small crock of oil, a table that had been notched along its edges in some primitive accounting, and reached for a bottle on the shelf: the taste of licorice cut the stench of the hut, the heat beneath the low ceiling. Boot took the opium smuggler's unlit lantern from its hook, hung up his own, and began to set the furniture straight, found some rags to mop the oil, not because he thought it was necessary, since the opium smuggler's price for the animal released Boot of anything approaching manners or concern or respect for anyone who lived on the island, but he cleaned and straightened the furniture anyway, not wanting to admit that it would have been all right even if he had set the house on fire.

Boot climbed the hill behind the opium smuggler's house and found the line and saw that there wasn't just the animal that Boot had seen the opium smuggler riding to town, but another as well, a little younger, a jackass that Boot had never seen on the island before. Boot sat on a stone and looked at the animals, realizing that the opium smuggler had heard (probably about three in the afternoon, and definitely from Thymos) about the need for an animal and had waited until dark (or more likely dusk, when it's most difficult to see) and then risked the boats and the disease and crossed to the mainland and bought a jackass.

The opium smuggler stood behind Boot and said, "Take the new one."

Boot nodded. The opium smuggler was gone. Boot took the animal from the line, held the lantern above its head, saw eyes that were as black and shiny as crude oil, examined its teeth, made sure its hooves weren't split, felt the stiff and dusty fur: its legs were salty from having been led from a beach to a boat. The animal's eyes watered. Boot put his fingers into the nostrils of the flinching jackass, examined the lines of crystalline fluid, all the more bright and clear against the gray fur.

It's a good animal. A year younger anyway. The man doesn't deal in trash.

The animal stood for the halter and saddle. Boot tied the bicycle to the saddle with a piece of blood-stiffened rope. The lantern was in the dust, and the animal's shadow seeped into the darkness beyond the yard. Boot held the lantern in one hand and the bottle and the lead rope in the other and began to walk toward the village, hearing the bicycle give and creak as the animal labored in the dust and then over the stones. The night was cool, as much drained of heat as light, and the air had become clammy as vapor condensed: mist clung to trees, stones, even the dust in the road, and in the light of the lantern each object had a glassine, brittle aspect. Boot stopped at a covered leaf, a glistening stone, and dismissed the entire phenomenon as another symptom of drink. He was frightened by the prospect of hallucinations, and fear of them had been his only reason for eating, since he knew that delirium was brought about by living on alcohol alone, starving the body to such an extent that it devoured itself. The brain was richest in protein. Boot stared at the animal and was amazed by what he led: an object that seemed junked and grafted, bizarre, half jackass, half machine. Boot and the lantern were connected, too, and the whole mess, fleshy and metallic, disjointed and swaying, was slouching toward town.

The monastery was pierced by two lanterns. Boot heard the wailing of Nicos, the oldest monk, who by almost any criterion should have been living with his coevals in the home for the aged. But the members of the monastery

74

looked after their own, partly out of concern, definitely because the monks were impeccably fatalistic: they despised the flesh and were fascinated by its decay. Nicos had visions of speckled creatures that hid in the trees and waited for him alone, wanting to eat his fingernails and hair, his teeth and nose. The other monks sat in the cell until Nicos said, "What the hell are you doing? Waiting to pick my bones. Get out. Get out. Leave an old man a little peace." The process was strictly private, since Nicos' condition was proof of the monks' beliefs.

Boot was pleased by the sound the hooves of the jackass made on the stones of the village street.

Let them hear it, because then they'll know I got one, and I didn't wait a day or a week, but I got one the same night.

Boot untied the bicycle and leaned it against the railing of Pavlos' taverna and then led the jackass along the quay and sat on the cold stone. He drank, reached every now and then for the animal's soft muzzle, slipped slowly and with relief from the stone wall to the quay itself.

2
Mara and Opium

The empty bottle clinked against the stone. The jackass pulled at the rope that was wrapped around Boot's arm. Boot lay curled against the stone, trying to keep the sun out of his eyes. Then he was fully awake and surprised: he saw blue sky, the shadows of the animal's legs stretching into dissolution, a fisherman at the end of the quay, and the woman from the hotel. She wore jeans, a blouse of some soft material, and sandals. She looked clean and tired.

"You've been asleep," said the woman.

"I wouldn't call it sleep," said Boot.

Boot felt his lip, dried blood cracking as he spoke. He tried to cover it with his hand.

"You're mumbling," said the woman.

"My lip's cut," said Boot. "I don't want you to see it."

Boot was struck by the difference between a drunken night and the stillness of the woman: it was like finding a table set with good silver, fine china, crystal, and flowers in the middle of a junkyard.

"It's almost five," said the woman. "The others, the fishermen, will be here soon."

"So what?" said Boot.

"There was some angry talk last night," said the woman.

"You speak Greek," said Boot.

"No," said the woman. "But I know angry talk when I hear it."

The animal gently nuzzled the woman. She pushed the furry and dusty head away.

Boot looked at the empty bottle, poked at it with one finger.

"I've got something to drink," said the woman. "If that's what you want."

Boot watched his shadow fall over the quay. Every object seemed to buzz. His knees felt as though they were filled with quivering fluid.

"You're an American," said Boot.

"New York," said the woman. "You?"

"California," said Boot.

They stared beyond the harbor, at the Turkish coast.

"Jack Daniel's," said the woman. "I've got a bottle in my room. I'll buy you a drink."

"My mouth," said Boot. "And clothes, too."

He looked at the torn and stained pants, the shirt stiffened with vomit and blood.

Goddamn, it wasn't just alcohol, but bits of myself as well.

"It's all right," said the woman.

"No," said Boot. "Wait."

Boot led the animal down the quay, away from the blank gaze of the fisherman, and tied it to the pole of the hotel awning. The woman had followed, walking on the other side of the jackass. She sat on a cold and damp chair.

There's got to be someone there, because the door and frame were torn from the plaster, and that couldn't have been fixed overnight. So someone had to watch, to stop the thieves.

Boot walked through the damp, bluish light, the shadows of the back street. *Jack Daniel's.* The shopkeeper sat in a chair before the ragged hole in the plaster wall. The chair was in the middle of the hole, and the shopkeeper slept with his legs apart, protecting the violated shop even in sleep. His snoring had a membranous quality that seemed concomitant with the hour and the empty street.

"I want to buy something," said Boot.

The shopkeeper woke quickly, startled by what was before him: Boot's face, the stench of vomit and anxiety, the distinct odor that comes from sleeping in a gutter, the dirty fist which held like a flower the brightly colored bills.

"A pair of pants and a shirt," said Boot.

The shopkeeper looked at the money and went into the shop, which was now as orderly as before, except there was a new department (if a store thirty feet long and ten feet wide can have a department) comprising bent, broken, and useless objects arranged as neatly as silver in a box lined with velvet. The shopkeeper brought a pair of white pants and a white shirt and wrapped them in brown paper and tied them with a piece of string. He gave the package to Boot.

"So you've found her," said the shopkeeper, "already."

"Here," said Boot, sticking a large bill into the shopkeeper's hand.

"I thought it would take longer," said the shopkeeper. He

looked at the bill, apparently not thinking of making change.

"You would," said Boot. "That's why you have a shop so far from the waterfront. I want my change."

The shopkeeper made change from his pocket.

The woman was smoking a cigarette, watching the boats come into the harbor. Those owned by the more prosperous fishermen made a steady popping sound as terminal engines labored in soft waters. The other boats were silent: men rowed with their backs to the quay, knowing that their catch would bring less, since the fishmongers would have already purchased most of the day's needs from the owners of the boats with engines. The woman brought the cigarette to her lips slowly, exhaled gently. The smoke seemed as milky as a prop wake.

Thymos' Renault was parked at the curb, and Thymos sat on the fender and watched the boats as they came to their moorings.

Thymos looked at Boot and frowned and said, "What have you bought?"

"Clothes," said Boot.

"From a store?" said Thymos.

Boot shrugged.

"I get out your way," said Thymos.

"I know," said Boot. "Maybe yesterday. About three."

"Maybe," said Thymos.

Thymos looked at the jackass.

"Between you and me," said Thymos, "where did you get that . . ."

Boot smiled and shook his head.

"I've never seen that jackass before," said Thymos.

Thymos looked once more at the jackass and then turned toward the quay, where fishermen were lifting bags of fish from their boats. The fishmongers were already yelling, belittling the catch, calling out the morning's litany of surly haggling. Thymos waited for a chance to sell liquor, a knife, a whetstone.

Boot said to the woman, "I'll use your shower. I'll look better when I'm clean."

They walked through the lobby of the hotel, which was new and modern: long leather couches, potted plants, large windows. The receptionist smiled at them, which surprised Boot, because even though the hotel was new, the customs of those who ran it were old. So it must have taken considerable effort on the part of the receptionist. There had been a great deal of opposition to building the hotel in the first place, since the islanders feared that the style of architecture alone would corrupt, that there was something about potted plants and stainless steel and leather furniture that carried new contagion, the spore of unwanted behavior.

The room was filled by the woman's presence: a faint odor, a few visible objects, a book, a brush, a bathrobe.

"Do you want this?" she asked. She brought the bottle of bourbon from the bathroom.

Boot looked out the window, listened to the sound of the waking harbor. Only the last of the catch remained: tag-end bitterness and final dismissals pierced the air. A fisherman shouted a blasphemy that was both thoroughly nihilistic and alive. The entire market was silent for a moment, but soon returned to its natural hubbub and tedium. Boot chuckled. The woman poured from the bottle of Jack Daniel's.

"Here," she said.

Boot drank from the hotel glass and said, "Thanks."

The entire floor of the bathroom was covered with red tile, and it sloped gently toward one corner where there was a bright drain. The stone had a fleshy quality, red tile and chrome: an Indian woman, nude, touched with silver. Boot stood under the running water, soaped once and then again, and realized that the door was open and that the woman was watching him. She sat on the bed with one leg drawn up, drank from the glass, ran her tongue along the rim where his lips had touched it. The sun rose from Turkey: the woman felt the light and warmth on her neck, shoulders, arms. Boot toweled, dressed, and came back into the room.

"You look like a peasant," said the woman. "A farmer."

From the terrace he saw that the animal was still tethered to the hotel awning. Fishermen sat on the other side of the street, gazing at the jackass and the door of the hotel. "I have what amounts to three hundred and fifty dollars," Boot said, "plus, from the island, fifteen hundred, profit on that jackass."

She said, "I have money."

"No," said Boot.

"We'll spend yours first then," said the woman.

"Three hundred and fifty dollars will last a long time," said Boot, "if we stay here."

She examined his features, arms, hands, the way his body moved, dwelled on his cut lip.

"It will heal," said Boot. "I didn't want to make a profit. It was a mistake."

"I liked watching you bathe," said the woman.

"Will you meet me this afternoon?" said Boot. "At the monastery, where I first saw you. I have to take the animal back. She's turning in harness."

"Who?" said the woman.

"An old woman. My landlord. I borrowed . . ."

"I know," said the woman. "There's a boy who speaks English."

Of course, only a child would tell her.

Boot sat and put on his shoes, glanced at the flesh of her hips pressed against the bed, her breasts in a sheer blouse, her hands, tapered fingers, narrow wrists. Her tongue touched the lip of the glass.

"Will you meet me?" said Boot.

She watched his hands spin laces into knots. There was dried slime, some leavings of the previous night, along the sole of one shoe. The sun struck her face, revealed her eyes: an extension of the brain, slick nerves, confined sky and shredded gold.

"It's a long walk for me," said Boot. "About one o'clock."

Boot stopped at the desk in the lobby and turned the register so he could read it. The man and woman behind the desk were more startled that Boot had spent the better part of an hour in the woman's room and didn't know her name than they were upset about being ignored. Boot admired the name: Mara. He ran a finger over the scratched paper.

Boot stood in the evaporating shadows, stroked the animal's face and neck, watched as the fishermen moved away from their boats. Some were walking toward Pavlos' taverna. The last of the bills and coins had changed hands and the fishmongers began carrying the catch away.

That's one nice thing about being a fisherman. You don't have to make excuses about drinking early.

Petros was already drunk.

"Well?" said Petros.

"Was the fishing good?" said Boot. *Did not bringing the body catch you any luck?*

Petros touched the animal.

"Where did you get it?"

"It's younger," said Boot. "At least a year. Maybe two. That should count for something."

Petros screamed. Boot stopped smiling. He stood and cupped the warm, smooth chin of the jackass.

"Where did you get it!" said Petros.

The jackass flinched and turned so that it stood between Boot and Petros. Boot put his hand on the animal's spine: it felt like small, connected spools beneath the skin and fur. Petros' face was as red as a bottle of blood.

Pavlos and Costas, Thymos, and some other shopkeepers approached them, walking as though they were simply enjoying the cool air, the quietness of the harbor after the day's business had been conducted. Boot greeted them, reached toward the animal with a proprietary gesture. Pavlos' son came, too, walking a little behind his father, appearing curious over Petros' anger and drunkenness: it wasn't the first time that Petros had raved, but it was the first time others had taken him seriously.

"I'll buy you a drink," said Pavlos.

"I don't want a drink," said Petros. "I want to know where he got it."

"No," said Boot. "You mean who."

Petros looked across the animal's backbone, but he kept his distance, apparently not wanting to touch the jackass. Its very presence was mysterious, and that fact alone was enough to make Petros dwell on his superstition.

"Yes," said Petros. "Who. I want to know who took our money."

"You're drunk," said Costas.

"Naw," said Petros.

The woman stood on the veranda, obviously intent on words she didn't understand.

"Here," said Boot. He held out a bill. "I'll buy him a drink."

The bill trembled in his hand. And then they were gone, and Boot stood next to the jackass, still holding the bank note. Costas and Pavlos walked slowly, laughed and joked, kept Petros from looking over his shoulder.

Boot began to follow his shadow: it stretched now toward the end of the island where he lived. He led the animal by the blood-stiffened rope.

She can't be angry, because she only had to turn in harness one day not to turn in harness for an extra year, because this animal, fine devil that it is, will last at least twelve months more than the other.

The sun was just above the horizon and Boot saw his distended shadow, moving in comic enlargement. He was curious about Ulla, because he had heard her speaking to the other jackass. She called it stupid and slapped it on the head with a stick. The animal had begun to jerk to one side whenever the woman picked up the branch. This made Ulla angry: she struck the animal on the other side of the head, and it worked. The animal stood still when the beating approached, since it didn't know from which side the blow would come. And even then the woman wasn't satisfied. She picked up the stick and the animal blinked and she hit it on top of the head, between the ears. This had happened in the morning: the slap and the honk of the jackass shattered Boot's alcoholic, hallucinatory sleep.

Boot stopped at the outskirts of the village, glanced at the hills around the harbor, the houses on them. They appeared festive and serene. Boot started along the road above the sea, from which he could see the Turkish coast, distinct in the clear air, sharply ridged, brownish. It seemed not peaceful, but desolate. The jackass stopped and honked, but Boot took little notice, since he was only aware of the heat, thoughts of the inner flesh of Mara's thighs, the sea that looked blue enough to stain swimmers.

Boot tied the jackass to the tree in the monastery courtyard and walked into the taverna. Lukas, the monk who had waited in the road for Boot, was gone, in prayer or fast, excused from looking after the monastery's business, and in his place was Yannis, a monk who was a little younger, a man whose face was raised by prominent bones and split by a nose as sharp and curved as the point of a scythe. He hadn't shaved, and he put out the tables and chairs in a manner both resentful and listless: his movements, the job itself, was a reminder of his lack of luck. There was only one vice permitted in the monastery, aside from self-hatred and mutilation of the soul, and since there was only one, it was practiced with a passion: gambling, card playing. And the one who lost the most not only lost whatever small amount he had been able to scrape together and hoard before the game, but a few days of freedom as well, since it was the heaviest loser who had to run the taverna until the next game. And judging by the expression that Yannis turned on Boot, a great deal had been lost, much more than Yannis could afford.

"It's early to be putting out chairs," said Boot.

Yannis glanced at Boot once, and Boot knew who had won the most.

"So," said Boot. "Maybe the devil plays cards."

The monk grunted and said, "I've thought of that."

"I'll bet," said Boot.

The winner must have been Nicos, hell's visionary and high roller, the one who's been seeing beasts.

Boot asked for a bottle.

"Sure," said Yannis. "Drink yourself to death."

There's only one place where he could have gotten enough to lose that much.

"The devil's lucky," said Boot.

Yannis turned on Boot, one hand trembling with rage and fatigue at the edge of his habit, and said, "A lot you know. The old bastard's got a screw loose. I don't think he even knows when he's bluffing. It ruins my game."

Boot paid for the bottle and walked to the gate.

Yannis said, "You won't be laughing long."

"Where did you sell it?" said Boot. "The ikon."

"What?" said Yannis.

"Relax," said Boot. "I don't want anything."

Yannis stood in the road. Boot walked, took small sips from the bottle, just enough to soothe irritated nerves, to enjoy the morning, the sound the jackass's hooves made on stone, the distant hiss of the sea. There was no one in the opium smuggler's yard: dust, chickens, a goat on a line, a rusted Renault station wagon. Boot stood in the light and listened: no dog. He waited a little more and then opened the door of Thymos' Renault, reached under the seat, and found it: St. George, paint and gold leaf, the spear and the serpent, scaled, green, and ruby-eyed, the killer himself, severe and sturdy, an instrument of God. It was at least five hundred years old, and it was against church law to remove an ikon from the monastery, against the laws of the island to take it to another, and in violation of the laws of the country to take it across a border.

So. Boot watched the sunlight strike gold. *It would bring a fair amount in Paris or New York. They're probably off in*

89

the bushes right now, bickering about a price. Because Thymos hasn't got what might be called irregular connections on the mainland. I can run up any debt with the opium smuggler and Thymos will have to spread the word that something's amiss, and he can't be too specific about it either, can't admit that he was about to sell an ikon. And the monk will keep his mouth shut, although he might tell a few people to be careful.

Boot put the ikon under his shirt and closed the door of the Renault. He led the jackass to the ridge, from which he could see his house: a small two-story building of plaster walls topped with a tile roof and trimmed with blue at the casements and door. The tile was the color of lips. In the fields below the house one figure worked, animated by the short strokes of a hoe. Boot led the animal into the valley. Ulla grasped the boom that was attached to the central gears of the well, and she walked in a circle, on earth smoother and harder than concrete, a surface composed of dirt and animal dung. She understood leverage as accurately as she counted on her knuckles: she grasped the boom at the point farthest from the well.

The water in the rusted pans flashed against the featureless brush on the hillside and dropped into the V-shaped trough that led to black earth. The woman grunted. Boot stood before her.

Ulla stopped and Boot saw a face as wrinkled and brown as a leaf of cured tobacco. It was animated by two features, a mouth of black teeth and eyes so blue they looked as though they had been filled with water from the sea.

"Here," said Boot.

The boom quivered. Ulla took the rope. She stood in the brush with a handful of dust and scrubbed at the stained fibers. Boot moved.

"It's too late," she said.

She soaked the rope in the last pan of the well and then stepped away from the surface of dung and earth and rubbed more dust into the fibers. At least the entire rope now had the same used and handled quality.

Boot reached for the saddle.

Ulla said, "No. If you had known how to clean it, you would have done so already."

Boot squatted and drank.

The woman cleaned the saddle and halter and looked at the animal.

"It's younger," said Boot.

"You think you have to tell me the ages of animals?" said Ulla.

She went over it closely, touching tendons, withers, neck, opening the mouth, peering into ears, rubbing a hand through the thick fur.

"At least a year," said Boot.

"Two," said Ulla.

She fitted the harness over the animal's head.

"You've met her," said Ulla.

"Yes," said Boot.

Ulla grunted and said, "They shouldn't have chased my animal that way."

"I tried to stop them," said Boot.

"I try in one hand and shit in the other," said Ulla, "which gets full first."

Ulla began to beat the animal, not with maliciousness, or any visible emotion. She did it with the extreme pragmatism that comes from a lifetime of getting all that is possible from everything, the last drop of oil from the can, the last seed from the sack.

She stopped and looked at Boot, and Boot said, "No. I

didn't bring the animal to be thanked." *Just as you don't thank a dinner guest for not blowing his nose in your linen napkin.*

Ulla made a noise that was neither pleasant nor ugly: it sounded as though someone were shaking a wooden bucket with some pebbles in it. Boot realized she was laughing.

"You can bring your slut here," said Ulla. "I don't mind."

Ulla beat the animal, drove it around the well: the pans creaked, water flowed toward the fields. Boot walked through the stunted arbor, the green and refreshing light, and climbed the steps to his house, or his part of it anyway, the upper floor. The basement room, which was carved out of the slope on which the house rested, belonged to the farmer's son, and he stayed there occasionally when he came to fish. During the day the farmer's son worked at the old people's home, emptying bedpans, looking after the feeble, playing with those whose bodies had outlived them.

Boot had three rooms: kitchen, study, and bedroom. The study had a cot and a window, and the window overlooked the fields, the cove, and the Turkish coast. Boot sat on the cot, leaned the ikon against the wall, and waited: his wind-up clock made a sound like a small mechanical horse trotting on cobblestones. He listened to the woman beating the animal, told time by the changing light in the room. Flies crawled on his skin. He changed clothes and waited and heard footsteps on his terrace and then a knock, tentative and discreet, at his door.

Hung over at noon.

Petros stood with his straw hat in his hand.

"I've got my boat," said Petros.

Boot nodded, watched the stricken eyes: Petros seemed to

be praying for the ease and quietness of his labor, when he waited for his nets to fill, when his boat seemed to be drifting not only on the sea but in the sky as well, moving slowly over stars reflected in still waters.

"I thought you'd be going someplace," said Petros.

"Where would that be?" said Boot.

Petros shrugged and moved the straw hat from one hand to the other.

"I don't know," said Petros. "But I could take you."

"Jesus," said Boot.

"What?" said Petros.

"I need a ride," said Boot. "You look like you need a drink."

Petros shook his head.

"It's easy to make a fool of me," said Petros. "But the others are smarter."

"Here," said Boot.

Petros eyed the bottle suspiciously.

"Go on," said Boot.

"I don't want it," said Petros.

Boot held the bottle. The jackass turned around the well. The old people labored in the fields.

"It wasn't that bad this morning," said Boot. "On the quay."

"It was bad," said Petros.

"You were drunk," said Boot. "You've been drunk before."

Petros took the bottle and swallowed hard.

"They ironed my head," said Petros.

Petros drank again. Boot listened to the hoes cutting black earth.

"We were friends," said the fisherman.

Boot shrugged.

"We drank and played backgammon at my place."

Petros' anger was as distinct as a bass drum.

Boot walked into the study, picked up the ikon, and said, "Here."

Petros was afraid to touch it.

"What's worse?" said Boot. "Getting drunk in public and asking questions or trying to steal this?"

"Who?" said Petros.

"It doesn't matter," said Boot. "I'm taking it back to the monastery. Will you give me a ride?"

There was a reflection on the wall from the ikon: it was diffused and mild, as though the sun had struck a pan of yellow, undulant fluid.

"It was in a corner," said Petros. "No one would have noticed."

The reflection fell across Petros' face.

"Here," said Boot.

"No," said Petros. "Look at my hands."

Petros had touched the ikon only with his lips.

"Do you miss your wife?" said Boot.

Petros said, "I don't cry anymore. Maybe I would have noticed."

"Maybe," said Boot.

They both drank.

"Don't worry," said Boot. "I'm the one who should be scared."

"In God's heart," said the fisherman, "I don't know anymore."

Boot took the ikon and the bottle and he and Petros walked through the fields to the beach, where Petros stopped and turned into the chapel, a small, squat building made of stone and beams covered with plaster. It was musty inside, filled with an odor like that in an unused warehouse.

There were nets and lines in one corner, and some burlap sacks where someone had slept. Cheap ikons hung on the wall opposite the door, honored not by the quality of the painter, but by the homage done before them, the time they had been in Petros' family. There were three of them, and they hung above and at the sides of a makeshift altar, a packing crate covered with clean burlap, sackcloth worn into elegance. Petros lit a candle and stuck it in a coffee can filled with dirt and gently touched each ikon with his lips, making the same piercing sound as before, one that embarrassed Boot because it verged on the untouchably private: a man might make love to a woman and then leave her, move away from the bed, kiss her gently and carelessly between the legs, and make such a sound. Boot stood next to the door and looked at the pile of nets.

Petros offered the ikons to Boot, simply by waiting a moment, by stepping away from them, and Boot looked at the nets, aware of the distance between Petros and the ikons, and shook his head and walked into the harsh noon light. The fields were quiet: the old people had gone to eat bread, oil, and olives and to take siesta.

They were in the boat. Petros stood between the gunwales and rowed with the heavy reluctance of old machinery. Boot stared at the strait and the mainland. He didn't ask about the engine: the sound of the oars in the locks, the diminutive wash and slap of water, were soothing.

"Where are you going to meet her?" said Petros.

"At the monastery," said Boot.

"I never swim," said Petros. "I hate it."

I wouldn't want to dig a grave, so why should he want to swim.

Boot stepped onto the ancient quay. Petros rowed and

Boot stared at the receding face: each feature was as blank and dumb as a coat hung on a hook.

Petros and the boat were pared by distance, cut away by the horizon's edge. Boot stared until his eyes watered and then climbed the switchback to the monastery.

Yannis sat on a chair.

"Here," said Boot.

Yannis blinked.

"Take it," said Boot.

It was odd to look at the ikon in the open air, outside brooding and ill-lighted space.

"No one knows," said Boot.

"Shame isn't less for being private," said Yannis.

Boot shrugged.

"Maybe you'll laugh a little longer than I thought," said Yannis.

"Maybe," said Boot. "Take it."

The ikon disappeared in the folds of Yannis' habit.

"I can't even thank you," said Yannis.

Boot looked at his shoes and said, "It wasn't done out of generosity."

Yannis brought bread, olives and oil, a piece of cheese as white as the plaster of the island's buildings. He brought two glasses as well, and then sat in the shade at a distance that was just enough to make conversation impossible. Bread turned golden in the oil was splashed with light. Boot ate slowly and watched the monastery's entrance: there was only the dry hillside framed by an arch.

Boot waited; the glass and the chair on the opposite side of the table were empty.

I'm only half the monster. The rest is scattered in the souls of those who live here. I couldn't have done it alone. And that's why they've got to be careful.

Yannis sat sullenly in the shade.

The chair squeaked on the flagstone: Mara sat opposite Boot.

"Are you drunk?" said Mara.

"Shit," said Boot.

"What?" said Mara.

"Nothing," said Boot. "Let's have a drink."

"I don't want one," said Mara.

She lit a cigarette, blew a quick stream of smoke into the air.

"Well?" she said.

"Christ," said Boot, "this isn't a guided tour."

"You look drunk," said Mara.

"If I want to be drunk, I'll be drunk. I'm not drunk."

"Fuck it," said Mara. "I'm going back to the hotel."

"Stop arguing," said Boot. "We're not married."

Mara smoked. Boot was quiet. Mara's thick and heavy and sunstreaked hair was loosely pinned in an onion-shaped Victorian style. Strands curled before her ears. Her tanned complexion shocked her features: eyes and lips seemed dark. There were freckles on her cheeks.

"I'll have a drink," said Mara.

Boot poured ouzo into the empty glass.

The table was distinct because it had been made by hand, by one person, so it was marred by small mistakes that were as dysfunctional as the personality and hands that made them.

Mara smiled and said, "You live alone."

Boot nodded, poured himself a small drink.

"Maybe it's just that you haven't had a woman in a long time," said Mara.

97

"No," said Boot. "Let's go for a swim."

She stood nude on the quay, her flesh as tanned and rich as the colors of the ancient stone. Her back was dimpled above the buttocks. Thighs, arms, calves, were smoothly muscled, slick, as though she had been waxed and oiled. She dangled her feet in the water. Boot sat next to her and she looked at him and laughed and said, "Don't be embarrassed," and took his penis in her hand. She saw in his eyes the reflection of her face, the sea beyond the quay. "I like holding you," she said.

She stopped touching him and saw them, too: Pavlos, Costas, Giorgos, and other fishermen and farmers and shopkeepers, standing on the terrace, drinking and smoking slowly, watching.

The stone was about a quarter of a mile offshore, midway between Samos and the mainland. It was whitish, streaked with geological markings, dark lines of sediment that ran at an oblique angle to the sea so that the entire stone had a sinking aspect, like a ship rising once out of the water before vanishing. It was the tip of some submarine peak, a danger to navigation, desiccated: it had no fresh water and was without the least shrub, a place that was avoided even by birds.

Mara sat on the white stone and breathed deeply. Boot sat beneath her, looked at the drops of water on her skin, her wet and pulled pubic hair. They lay side by side in a smooth hollow. Boot had his hand beneath her side, could feel the heat of the stone, the humidity from the evaporating water. He gently opened the lips between her legs with his tongue. The interior flesh, moist and sanguine, seemed all the more delicate because of the white stone, the pure nakedness of the place, the light. Boot sucked at a strand of her hair. Their bodies dried, were left with salt marks. Boot licked them away from her hips, from beneath her breasts, saw the whitish pattern of the down above her knee where she hadn't shaved. The stone, the air, made them seem vulnerable, temporal, joyful. Beneath Mara there was a stain, a mark that was drying, whitening in the sun.

Mara touched Boot, her juices on him, ran one finger along his penis, and then licked it. Boot stood behind her: she seemed made by a careful hand. Her buttocks rested easily on the stone. Boot thought of a chair in an ancient theater: it was two thousand years old, carved from marble, and it was still the most comfortable chair he had ever sat in. They walked, Mara's flesh undulating and stiffening with the shock and relaxation of movement. The slime on the stone just beneath the waterline seemed bizarre, alien from dry rock. Mara's hair hung to her shoulders, covered the upper part of her back. Boot bathed with her, watched her body foreshortened by the glassine water, the fish darting together as though they were all on strings pulled by the same hand. They sat on the stone again. Boot looked at the stain they had made, now more white than the rock itself. The monastery looked like a calcimine chip on the hillside. Boot put his head against Mara's thigh, hoped that when she moved he could hear the tendons hiss beneath the skin, but heard only the popping of the engine of a fisherman's boat.

"They're coming to pick us up," said Boot.

She looked at him.

"There," he said, pointing over the distance they had swum. "That boat."

"I'm naked," she said.

"You still don't understand," said Boot.

"I understand I don't want to be made into a spectacle," said Mara.

Boot walked down to the water again and turned and saw Mara trying to cover herself, crossing her legs, folding her arms across her breasts.

Boot waited for the boat and then said to Petros, "Give me her clothes."

Petros pulled the boat closer and handed Boot the woman's clothes and then Boot's own.

"Here," Boot said to Mara.

He walked back to the water and waded and said, "Give me the bottle. And the pitcher of water."

Petros smiled and handed Boot the bottle and the pitcher that had been on the table of the monastery, and Boot drank from the bottle and then from the pitcher. Mara drank, too, and Boot said, "Put on your clothes. He's waiting."

Boot dressed, sat with the bottle, gestured toward the island, and said, "It's not that it's too much for people."

"What?" said Mara. She pulled on her pants.

"You're very pretty," said Boot.

It isn't too much for people, because they love what defies them, and if the farmers, fishermen, and shopkeepers could string the island up and slaughter it and drink its blood, they'd do it. But the island, the harshness of it, won't let them.

"I'm glad," said Boot.

He looked at the hollow, the stain, a bit of salt on Mara's neck.

Mara pulled her blouse over her head and said, "So what."

Boot stood in the sunlight, holding the bottle and the pitcher.

"Maybe glad has nothing to do with it," said Mara. "Maybe I just wanted to swim out to a rock and get fucked. Maybe that's all."

"Maybe," said Boot. "Don't put your sandals on. We've got to wade."

Petros held the boat against the rock with the oars. The engine idled.

Boot helped Mara into the boat and then climbed in after her. They sat in the front and watched the rock recede. Petros held the tiller, the end of which was as shiny as a piece of glazed pottery.

"Don't be angry," said Boot.

"How could I be?" said Mara. "You've got the market cornered."

Petros didn't understand, but he laughed anyway, made a sound that was barely audible over the hammering of the engine, the old and unique piece of machinery that Petros would have kept even if he had money to buy another: it was all that remained of his wife.

Mara took the bottle and drank, pulled the liquor into her mouth; bubbles rose in the bottle. Boot saw the water rising in her eyes. Boot passed the bottle to Petros, and Petros drank and laughed and passed the bottle back.

"You have beautiful hands," said Boot.

"I've been told that before," said Mara.

Mara sat in the stench of oil and gasoline and gazed at the coast: it quivered in the heat of the engine. Every board in the boat vibrated. Mara's jeans were tight and she wore no underwear. A dark oblong stain appeared at the seam between her legs. The boat bumped gently against the quay. Petros had an expression that was more vicious than he himself realized: he smiled genuinely, as though he were chauffeur at some event of personal happiness.

The terrace was empty. The shopkeepers and farmers were gone and the monks were taking siesta or playing cards. Boot and Mara stood in the road. Mara pushed the car keys into Boot's hand. He liked the smell of new leather, the sense of enclosure in a precise machine, racing by frugal land that was the antithesis of speed and factories.

The radio picked up only Turkish stations; they listened to squawking violins, songs of lament. They were in the valley, in the center of the island, where the fields were most rich (or least unfertile): wheat and vines and olive trees were pressed and spread by the movement of the car.

Mara asked the usual questions.

"And?" said Mara.

"I don't remember much more," said Boot.

"What do you remember?" said Mara.

"Women," said Boot, "and hangovers."

There was no land offshore, simply a blurred horizon where water turned into air. It was the hottest time of the day. Eyes ached: white plaster seemed pure and new, as though the buildings had been cast rather than built. The taverna was ten feet from the waveless water.

They ate cheese and bread, with a little oil, and olives, small meatballs and cucumber and tomatoes; a fish, a large one for each, baked in lemon juice and garlic; lamb, cut from a turning spit; eggplant that had been cut into slices and fried so there was a light crust on the outside but a luxurious softness within. The eggplant was covered with a paste made of garlic. Mara smiled and spoke. They drank cold retsina. They ate melon and were done.

The car moved quickly over its own shadow. The road looked as though it were a narrow reservoir for quicksilver; Boot watched the reflection of the end of the valley in the heat. Mara played with the radio, switched stations, finally shut it off again and said, "Christ. Maybe I picked you up just to hear a little English."

* * *

On the waterfront Pavlos and Costas and the other shop-keepers and fishermen acknowledged and greeted Boot and Mara by a slight suspension of movement. The shopkeepers wore dark glasses and the fishermen and farmers squinted.

"Did you have a good swim?" said the clerk behind the desk.

They climbed the marble stairs. The acoustics of the stair-well were faulty: an echo struck and lingered. Footfalls had the aspect of an object between two mirrors.

Boot sat in the chair near the terrace and poured himself a drink, held the glass to the harbor: dark earth and air, bourbon and blue sky.

"You drink too much," said Mara.

"You've said that," said Boot.

"You're still doing it," said Mara.

"You like opium," said Boot.

"I've never had it," said Mara.

"I like liquor better," said Boot. "It loosens my tongue."

"Who have you been talking to?" said Mara. "Yourself?"

Boot sipped his drink. Mara took off her clothes and sat on the bed. Boot's chair was opposite her: he could smell the salt on her skin, the beginning of a rich and cloying odor, almost chocolaty, deep and strong, internal, the reek of decay that nourishes, compost and marsh. Woman's flesh, the slight roll of hip, pressed against the bed. Her arms were covered with bleached down.

The film of liquor covered the glass, distorted the harbor, sky, Mara.

She leaned against a pillow, rested a heel against the edge of the bed, laid the back of an ankle across the arm of Boot's chair. She had not always sunbathed nude; there was a brief shadow over her hips. Boot touched a blue vein, but was

103

unable to tell whether the pulse was beneath her skin or in his finger. There was a used quality about her, but it enhanced rather than diminished her beauty, since it made her features appear faintly roughened, or diffused, or anyway changed, as though her body had absorbed not only injury but the kernel of vitality in abuse. Boot sipped his drink, kissed the inside of her thigh, left a little liquor there, licked it briefly and blew on the moist spot.

"We'll bathe together," said Mara.

She stepped into the bathroom, turned on the water, stood on one leg to avoid the stream, adjusted the temperature.

There is one thing a woman can never understand: the simple fact of her beauty: she may debase it, use it to manipulate and demand, may debase it further by taking a conscious place in some grisly pecking order, but she can never understand the gift of it, the aura that surrounds it.

Mara's flesh was slick and shiny, animated by the spray and her moving and soaped hands.

"You're lovely," said Boot.

"No," said Mara. "Don't tell me anything about the way I look. It's like a broken record."

Boot finished his drink, glanced out the window at the harbor, and realized the debt would be paid, with interest, knew that Pavlos, Costas, the fishermen and farmers and shopkeepers, would only have to wait. But the waiting wouldn't be blind and deaf, since the islanders' understanding went deeper than the knowledge of patience: they lived with the ruins, that slowly dissolving pile of stones, and they knew, although they could never admit of it, that those stones were the physical embodiment of the erotic quality of their history, the connection of the grubby, the stark, the tedious, with richness and some splendor, intelligence and beauty. And even if these things dwelled in the nerves or flesh or whatever there is below mind, the islanders knew the value of transitory pleasure, if only because the smallest one was charged by twelve or more hours in the field, the agonized grubbing after a two-cent profit. The ruins were a monument to transitory success. And there wasn't a soul on the island who would dare lift so much as a finger to stop the inevitable decay, and not a soul who felt anything but the most complicated mixture of regret and relief when the deterioration had noticeably progressed.

Boot stood under the shower: the red stone, bright fixtures, Mara's glazed flesh, were distorted by water. Her torso seemed encased in a drawn and moving membrane, pierced twice by sunned nipples. The room was struck by a stark odor. Mara opened a leg to the shower, reached into herself with drawing motions, apparently immune to her own flesh. She seemed to be tearing something from between her legs. Mara faced Boot and he tasted the water on her breasts and stomach, touched the inside of her thigh with his fingers, found between full lips, wet and curly hair, a channel as slick as oiled silk. Boot kneeled and put his mouth between her legs, felt her nails on his shoulders: he sucked at inner lips, a tight, shifting ridge, tasted her, the island's water pierced by minerals. There was a lack of something in the way she tasted, an emptiness, or lack of difference that compelled: it was a mixture of closeness and surprise, a taste no different from Boot's own mouth. The drain sucked at Boot's heel. Her skin seemed taut beneath the easy sheath of water. He sat on the stone floor, felt the gentle and wet bobbing of her thighs and buttocks against his hips, breasts barely touching his chest. Mara's sunstruck hair splashed against stone. She stared at the grasping and protuberant flesh between her legs. Boot watched her tanned shoulders against billows of vapor, thick mist cut by light on chrome. She opened as though flesh and bone could spread, seemed to be floating over him, except for the surprise of bump and end, a hard internal ring. Boot kissed her underarms, touched a wet breast, the muscles moving in her hips and back. Mara put her hands on Boot's shoulders, let the water fall between them and over her groin. She slipped, touched Boot's hair, the tile behind his head.

She said, "Honey."

"What?" said Boot.

"Nothing," said Mara.

Boot felt immediately strange and ridiculous under the running water. The muscles in his legs danced with the ashy leavings of excitement. They rinsed. Mara turned off the water. Boot touched her and said, "You're pretty here."

He put his hand between her legs.

"Here," he said.

"I thought it was all the same," said Mara.

"No," said Boot.

Boot took a towel and went into the bedroom, poured himself a drink, and watched her frown, her stance of annoyance.

"It's hard to get that," said Mara, pointing to the Jack Daniel's.

"I'll go downstairs and get a bottle of local stuff," said Boot.

"Why don't you do that?" said Mara.

Boot pulled on the pair of white pants.

"Wait," said Mara.

She bent at the waist and began to towel her hair. The room smelled of the soap and the island's clean air.

"You can have it," said Mara. "It doesn't matter what you drink as long as you're going to."

He sipped from the glass, stepped onto the terrace: farmers and fishermen sat in the taverna, turned, as though on cue, when Boot could be seen. The nets were spread to dry. Water was cut by stone.

"Still waiting," said Boot.

Mara toweled her hair.

The desk clerk smiled. Boot and Mara walked into sunlight: the harbor was flat and smooth, appearing in the heat to be slowly cooling glass, its surface creased only by the wake of a fishing boat. The waterfront was blocked with vital colors, oranges, blues, greens, pigments that had withstood the island's countless seasons. Heat rose from the stones.

Costas, Pavlos, Petros, some other shopkeepers and fishermen, sat at a group of tables under the orange awning of Pavlos' taverna. They drank Coca-Cola and lemonade. Dice clicked on the backgammon board. Chips moved. Mara and Boot took a table close by. Giorgos was there, too, since he was passing through the town, halfway through the day's labor, midway between his scattered plots of land.

"Drinks," said Boot to Pavlos' son. The boy looked at Boot without interest.

"Good day," said Giorgos. He took off his hat and bowed to Mara. Giorgos spoke nervously, as though to an association he would not be allowed to join. Boot saw the number of empty glasses in front of Giorgos' chair, knew, too, why he had been allowed to run up such a debt in one afternoon: the farmer's duplicity evaporated. He had been one of those who stole, or who made a spectacle of Mara's nudity. Mara gazed at the harbor.

"Good day," said Giorgos.

Boot looked at Costas and Pavlos, Petros, and the others,

caught each face momentarily, and said, "Why doesn't someone buy him another drink?"

Giorgos reached toward Mara and said, *"Mouni."*

"What?" said Mara.

"Cunt," said Boot.

"You wouldn't know," said Boot to Giorgos. "She's not an animal."

Giorgos' face broke: the wrinkles became more pronounced. He shook his head.

"A goat," said Boot.

"What?" said Costas.

"He'll tell you," said Boot, "if you buy him another drink. Look at his face."

Costas stared and said, "Yes."

Giorgos' complexion, a farmer's tan, took care of shame: only his eyes watered. He retreated, knocked over a chair, kept his gaze away from the others.

"I don't do it," said Giorgos.

"Don't do what?" said Boot.

"What you're going to say I do," said Giorgos.

The taverna was filled with laughter.

"What's this about a goat?" said Petros.

"Nothing," said Giorgos.

"I'll . . ." said Boot.

"No," said Giorgos. His eyes were filled with pleading for the shred of dignity he had been able to maintain in spite of being a poor farmer whom the townspeople despised, took advantage of, and laughed at.

"All right," said Boot. "I don't know anything about it."

Giorgos was apologizing, first to Mara and then to Boot. He took a drink and led his jackass down the quay. Costas and Pavlos looked suspiciously at Boot.

"What was it?" said a shopkeeper.

"Nothing," said Boot. "I'm sure you've done worse."

The shopkeeper's complexion could afford the luxury of blushing. The taverna was filled with laughter again.

Boot said to Costas, "How was business this morning?"

Costas shrugged and said, "More gossip than money."

"But maybe more business than usual," said Boot. "Because what better place to gossip than a store?"

"Yes," said Costas. "Maybe so."

Costas smiled.

The boy brought drinks.

"My father sends them," said the boy. "With his compliments."

"To your father, then," said Boot, tossing off the clear liquor in one draught. "Ask him to send another."

The boy brought another. A bit of breeze cut the rising heat, the smell of sweating bodies.

"We were discussing . . ." said Costas.

The drink stopped halfway between the table and Boot's mouth.

"No matter," said Pavlos.

Bullshit.

Dice clicked. Costas moved the chips on the backgammon board. Chains clinked in the harbor. Mara watched Boot's face and then looked at the others.

"Yes?" said Boot.

"This disease," said Costas. He shrugged, touched his dark glasses, glanced toward the mainland. "People don't get a chance to enjoy themselves . . . they're afraid to get together in public where . . . well . . ."

"Well," said Boot, "where they can catch something. But people here should be more accustomed because of the lepers."

Boot pulled his hand into a stumpy claw.

109

"The lepers," said Pavlos. "Yes, you're right."

"It's only a matter of fifteen hundred," said Costas.

Costas' stunted, mercenary fingers rested on the table: the nail of the little finger on his right hand was long and tapered, bodily proof that Costas did no manual labor.

"Which fifteen hundred?" said Boot.

"We have a festival every year at this time," said Petros.

Costas glanced at him once, and Petros was quiet.

"Which fifteen hundred?" said Boot.

"Does it matter?" said Costas.

"I guess not," said Boot.

Shit, I have to think, they only have to breathe.

Costas sighed, rubbed thumb against index finger, gazed at Boot through smoked lenses, and said, "Do you have fifteen hundred?"

"You mean," said Boot, "did I pay for the jackass?"

"Yes," said Costas, "you could be right."

Boot laughed.

"Drink up," said Pavlos.

Mara's hair was dry and full. She wrapped a strand around a tapered finger; it looked as though she wore a band of streaked gold, a ring of her own making, emblem of her marriage to herself. She looked at the men in the taverna with a mixture of curiosity and contempt.

"I have fifteen hundred," said Boot.

"Well?" said Pavlos.

"There's a traveling carnival on Ikaria," said Costas, "and they could come for our festival, but, as I told you, people don't like to get together in public."

"They're not doing well," said Boot.

"The disease," said Petros, as if it were a rival whose attractions could only be seen behind closed doors.

The breeze stopped and the heat was more noticeable: it

felt like some clinging membrane. Boot thought of Mara's thighs, her inner flesh, as smooth as lightly blown air.

Boot sipped his drink. The islanders waited.

"I understand," said Boot. "They need a guarantee."

"For the first day," said Costas. "The second is theirs. They've got to make something."

Petros squinted even in the shade, so it wasn't his eyes that struck Boot, but his entire face: the skin looked like it had been cut from a leather jacket.

"Fifteen hundred," said Petros.

Boot sipped his drink and was aware of memory: heat and thighs, symmetrical lips holding in the space between limbs a dipped and muscled ring.

"I understand," said Boot.

"You see," said Costas.

Pavlos smiled. Petros smiled.

"They have a geek," said Petros.

The chairs squeaked. Costas wiped perspiration from his brow and neck with a folded handkerchief. Dice clicked on the backgammon board.

"So," said Mara, "you've struck a bargain."

Boot felt like the heir of that first man who decided he didn't have the time or the energy or whatever to crack someone over the head and take a coveted object, but who did have the time and energy and shrewdness to offer something less esteemed in trade.

"Yes," said Boot. *Fuck it, let them try.* "It has something to do with the carnival."

Costas, Pavlos, Petros, and the rest looked at him: each face was as blank as an empty plate.

Boot shrugged and said, "All right. Where do I send the money?"

"No," said Costas. "The festival starts in two days."

111

"I could write a letter," said Boot.

Costas drank Coca-Cola, seemed oblivious to the flies that fed on his perspiration.

"No," said Costas. "Because even if it got there in time, the man who owns the carnival can't read. So he wouldn't know what to do with the money."

It's the profit, that five hundred.

"How much is the passage to Ikaria?" said Boot.

"A boat leaves tomorrow," said Costas.

"How much?" said Boot. He looked at the smoked lenses, the filed and pampered nail. "About five hundred?"

"Approximately," said Costas.

"I'll bet," said Boot.

"She can pay her own way," said Petros, pointing to Mara.

"Sure," said Boot.

"You see," said Costas. "He understands."

Each face opened and closed as quickly as a heart valve. The shopkeepers and fishermen went back to their back-gammon, ouzo, and Coca-Cola.

"With my father's compliments," said the taverna keeper's son. He put two more drinks on the table.

Mara drank, too, and Boot saw her face and hair against the cluttered edge of the harbor, the flat water. Siesta broke: the streets filled with people.

"I like traveling by ship," said Mara.

Mara brought the car. They drove to the end of the quay and Boot got out and walked to the barred window of the steamship company. The clerk wore dark glasses even though he sat in the shade: he had white skin, the complexion of a whore or a vampire.

"I have them," said the clerk.

"Five hundred apiece," said Boot. He slid the money under the bars. Mara sat in the car. The sunlight was filled momentarily with the sound of violins and wailing voices. Breezes carved the open sea. Waves, diminished by distance, flashed like silver coins.

"Wait," said the clerk.

"Wait?" said Boot. "Wait for what?"

"Your change," said the clerk.

He pushed two coins under the bars.

Goddamn. They've included a piece of bread and a drink.

The clerk returned to a condition of practiced immobility.

Mara drove. Boot slouched against the door. As Mara turned her head, other personalities seemed to command her features. It was startling, since it implied that she would become more striking as she grew older, that age and experience would only make more lush what was already apparent.

Dust overtook the car.

Mara opened the door and began to walk above the dirt road, through the pebbled and white-rocked landscape, toward terraced fields filled with weeds. Boot watched his shadow slide over the stones and dried grass. Wild oats burrowed into Mara's skirt. Boot took off his shirt and spread it in the weeds. Mara sat on the shirt, felt the sun on her nude skin. Boot ran his tongue along her hairline. She pushed him back, out of her, and said, "Lie back, look at the weeds or a rock or the scorpion I saw," and took his penis in her mouth. She bit gently and said, "Do you want to come in my mouth?"

Boot looked at her, the back of her head over his stomach, and said, "No."

He leaned on his elbows, fingered the tendons in her neck,

smelled their deep and mutual odor, watched her tanned flesh moving against the brownish grass, the sky, the flash of the undersides of the olive leaves.

They felt perspiration dry, the drops of semen and fluid congeal.

"How long has it been since you've had a woman?" said Mara.

"Almost a year," said Boot.

Boot picked pieces of blond straw from Mara's hair, sucked the blood from a scratch on her leg. She shook her head, opened her thighs to the sun. Boot licked the light stubble under her arms.

Boot looked through the grass and saw two women dressed in the clothes of perpetual mourning, dresses of a worn black material, standing next to the car. They had jackasses with them, and the women spoke and gestured and scanned the fields on the uphill side of the road.

"Come on," said Boot.

The islanders would have preferred me to have taken the most beautiful of the year's crop of pubescent daughters, cranked her up on ouzo, and fucked the piss out of her rather than what I've done.

"Maybe they'll go away," said Mara.

"No," said Boot. "They'd wait all night and then search the weeds to see where they've been flattened."

Mara dressed.

"They're making me feel like a slut."

One of Mara's cheeks was red, colored by mild abrasion. She picked straw from Boot's shirt. Boot took a strand of her hair, drew its end into a sharp point, and tickled her ear. She pushed him away.

Boot and Mara stepped onto the road. Boot cupped the

mouth of one of the jackasses, stroked the fur, and said to the women, "Good afternoon."

"Good afternoon," said one of the women.

The other nodded. Boot smiled.

"If you're in a hurry," said Boot, "we could offer you a ride."

"No," said one, "we're not in a hurry."

The women were almost identical: age had made them twins. Boot saw the elongated reflection of the jackasses on the fender of the car.

"I could lead the jackass," said Boot.

"No," said the same one. "It's better this way."

"Good," said Boot.

Mara smiled without saying a word and got into the car.

"She's very pretty," said the woman. She pointed to Mara. Her hand had spent so much time in the soil it looked more like a root than flesh.

Mara started the engine. The jackasses flinched, and even the women seemed frightened by the sound for a moment. Boot listened to the radio. The animals and the women disappeared, screened by the dust turned up by the wheels of the car.

The silence of the monastery seemed to pierce the landscape. The building was isolated on the precipice above the sea, so patently made by human hands, yet startling in the apparent lack of activity behind its walls. It seemed deserted rather than still.

"Is there more road?" said Mara.

She glanced at the dwindling slash in the island's side.

Boot laughed and said, "Yes. About a mile. Park the car there."

Mara drove and said, "This isn't a road. It's not even a goat path."

Dust surrounded them, spread through the olive trees, drifted through the opium smuggler's yard.

"I can taste it," said Mara. "I can feel the grit in my teeth. You don't live here."

"No," said Boot.

They walked through the yard, the slowly settling dust. The only sounds were the flap and thump of chickens' wings, the barking of a dog. The opium smuggler sat under a tree. Boot and Mara stopped in front of him. The opium smuggler didn't move a muscle, or make the least acknowledgment of them, being (as in most things) aloof, having purchased Boot's invisibility with one jackass, whatever the market price. So he stared toward the mainland, the slowly rotting crops, the unrealized profits rising in the heat. The disease gave him nothing to do: he waited, broke the vigil only for drink or to sire a bastard. But even these respites had grown stale, since they were an escape from something that for the present, at least, no longer existed: the early-morning crossings, the laconic dealings, precious adrenaline.

"Is he blind?" said Mara.

"No," said Boot. "Come on."

They walked through the yard and then to the top of the ridge, where there were large stones, white boulders, hot and glaring protrusions in the stubborn growth, yucca and cactus. Mara looked at Boot's house, the small flat valley that was entirely cultivated, quilted with irregular but contiguous plots of land. Boot's house, the farmer's, Petros' lean-to, the small church, seemed distinct and pure against the lushness of the land, the crystalline water of the bay.

Ulla said, "He's a good one."

116

The jackass turned the boom quickly around the well. The chains clinked. Pans of water rose to the fields. Nails had been driven into the harness: if the animal stopped or stepped backward, its skin was pierced. There were drops of blood on the circular path of dung and earth.

"I thought so," said Boot.

"Your rent's due," said the woman.

Ulla looked at Mara, and Boot said, "Go up to my house. The door's open." Mara climbed the path, walked through the arbor, and into the house.

"She's a pretty slut," said Ulla, "your slut."

Boot looked at her and then at the land beyond, part of what had been her dowry, probably the least part, since the other had been a watch her father had brought from India, where he had gone to make his fortune in trinkets and deceit. The watch had belonged to an officer in the British army, and the officer lost it in a card game to a clever Indian. The Indian cheated, so after taking the officer's pay and watch he took the officer's life as well. Ulla's father never told his wife or Ulla or anyone else for that matter how he had come into possession of the watch, but whenever he told the story of the card game and the officer he laughed like an idiot: the only spoils of five years in India were malaria, the clap, passage home, and the watch. So when Ulla's prospective husband first came to the fields he looked at the land and shook his head and took Ulla's father aside and said, That's not much land, and it's a long way from town. Ulla, then a woman of twenty-eight (who already nourished the seed of the aged creature she became), looked at her father and began to cry, not in such a way that the prospective husband could see (because she cried without tears or movement), but in a way that her father had noticed before, when other men had come to look at the land, had gauged the distance from the fields to town and the age of the daughter, and had said, It's not much land, and it's a long way from town.

So this time Ulla's father said, Wait, and went into the house and opened a trunk covered with peeling stickers, each one prized almost as much as the ikons in the monastery, and carefully removed the lace shirt and pistol and plates and finally the watch. It was wrapped in yellowing tissue paper. Ulla's father took the watch to the fields and said, Here. He let the watch swing by its chain. The prospective husband, the man who now tilled the fields and who was virtually indistinguishable from Ulla, looked at the watch and was clearly stunned, because its existence had become almost legendary, the story having been told so many times in tavernas that the physical evidence had come to seem as remote and fantastic as the stories of India: that men had black semen and women no pubic hair. He looked at the land and the aging daughter and said, When do you want the wedding? And Ulla's father said, A week from Sunday. Ulla was stunned by the watch, too, since she had seen it only twice before, when her brother was born and when her mother had died, and stunned moreover because she was going to be married in a week, and all because of the watch, which seemed more powerful than any of the ikons she had prayed before. The prospective husband said, Yes, a week from Sunday. Bring the watch.

"A pretty slut," said Ulla to Boot.

"Yes," said Boot. "Does your watch still work?"

Ulla's face twitched once but that was all; she stood in front of the well's turning gears, the jackass, the land where her husband worked.

"Here's your rent," said Boot, dropping the bills on the

dirt and then walking through the arbor and up the path to his house.

Mara stood in the kitchen and looked at a shelf which was a bank of sorts, a drunk's nest egg against lack of money or supply; it now held four bottles of ouzo.

"What's that?" said Mara.

"For emergencies," said Boot. "Tired?"

"Dirty," said Mara. "And sore. A stabbing pain."

On Boot's terrace there was a shower, or a contraption that passed for a shower. It looked like a moonshiner's still with legs: on a wooden frame there were two oil drums, connected by a pipe and having on one side a showerhead. Boot used two five-gallon cans to fill the drums with water from the well.

"Take off your clothes," said Boot.

Mara stood under the water. The terrace was visible from the fields. Ulla and her husband worked with their hoes. The jackass moved around the well.

"How come they don't watch?" said Mara.

"I paid the rent," said Boot.

The water was warmed by the heat of the day. Mara's skin was wet, her body edged by sunlight. Boot watched her raise an arm, and was amazed that he had been inside her.

The water ran out. Mara and Boot sat in chairs beneath the small arbor in front of Boot's door. It was late afternoon. The sea and the sky were the same color, and the landscape was touched by a mild, retracting light, as soft to stone and earth as private skin to fingertips.

"No," said Mara. "I'm sore."

"I am, too," said Boot, "but that doesn't mean I can't touch you."

"Maybe later," said Mara.

They could hear the steady chopping sounds of the hoes

in the fields. Boot saw Petros' boat in the cove. Ulla went to the beach and waited and then Petros spoke.

I'm glad I don't have to read lips.

Mara got into bed. Boot gathered her underwear and said, "I'll wash them and hang them out to dry. That way you can spend the night here and we won't have to go back to the hotel before the boat in the morning."

"Whatever," said Mara. She turned toward the wall, exposing her finely muscled back to crimson sunlight. Her legs curled gently toward her buttocks.

Boot took the clothes to the end of the terrace where there was a tub. He brought the scrub board and soap from the house and then tossed the bucket into the well. It landed upside down on the water, made a noise in the bricked hole that sounded like the hoof of a horse on pavement. Boot was glad to touch Mara's clothes.

Ulla saw him working and said, "So you're already a servant."

Boot rinsed the underwear.

"She wears pretty things," said Ulla. "Such pretty things."

Ulla stared for a moment at the fabric.

"Here," said Ulla.

She put a jug of wine on the steps of the terrace. The wine had come from the plants over which Ulla and her husband labored. It was a gift of some luxury, because the grapes from this season weren't ripe and everyone on the island was rationing the wine that was left from the previous season. And especially luxurious on this day, when Boot knew that the old man and Ulla wanted to sit before their empty fireplace and drink until they saw the demons that had been chasing the old monk around the monastery: the old man and Ulla were close enough to the grave to believe in almost anything, Nicos' visions, the horrors of alcoholic hallucinosis, the omens of crops and tides, the portents of a deformed creature caught in a net, the casting of the sorceress who lived on the other side of the island, the one who had treated Petros' oozing sores and who, when Boot first arrived, offered a spell to keep the scorpions away from him.

"So," said Boot, "Petros spoke to you."

"Here's the wine," said Ulla.

Boot squeezed the water out of the delicate underwear and was afraid for a moment that he had twisted the fabric too much, that he had ruined it.

"And this, too," said Ulla.

She held the watch by its chain. Boot put out his wet hand and took it.

"It's a good watch," said Ulla. "And it still runs."

Boot looked at the fine engraving, as sharp as when the watch had left the jeweler's hand.

"Keep it," said Ulla.

Years of stooping had given her the posture of one who was about to pitch forward into a hole. Ulla turned and walked through the fields and up the path that led to her house. The old man was waiting for her there with a jug of wine. Boot listened to the climbing footsteps, but that was all he heard: the old man didn't even ask about the watch.

Boot hung up the clothes and walked into the house, undressed, and lay next to Mara. Her back and legs were defined by white sheets. Boot could smell the island's air in the cloth: it was charged with the scent of earth and vegetation after rain. Boot held the watch and listened to the ticking, a sound that had the resonance of years, the passage to India, the partings and anger and blood it had been witness to, the days it sliced in the Indian heat. Each tick was rich: a man takes off his watch and puts it on a table next to his bed, so this one had probably absorbed into its gears and works the Englishman's mute whores, Ulla's father's case of the clap, and the old man's and Ulla's grunted and muddled fumblings, their childmaking, the mixing of their blood. Boot put the watch next to Mara's shoulder and stared at her skin as it slowly changed color in the day's tag-end light, until the skin was precisely the same color as the watch itself, as though the glob of metal were some recently removed growth. Boot put the watch on the pillow and touched Mara, who was now half asleep and responded sluggishly, rolling toward him and dropping an arm on his shoulder. Boot looked at the watch and gently bit her ear and neck, kissed the inside of her forearm, slowly touched, opened, pushed into ringed and slick space. Mara's hair was splayed over the pillow. Boot pushed the watch into it: the metal looked as though it had been engendered there. Each strand was as delicate and sharp as the lines on the engraved surface. Boot warmed the watch in his hand, pushed it into Mara's neck, ran it along her side, let the chain drop momentarily across a nipple gathered into itself. He left the watch at his side, pressed his cheek and ear against her neck and shoulder and looked at the gold, waited while the light changed the color of the watch and Mara's skin, thought of spreading gears and levers and springs and jewels, too, throughout the bed: he would find one piece and then another, each moist and damp, a bit under her arm, beneath a breast, at the side of a hip, a jewel between her legs.

The watch was next to Mara's moving hip; the muscles beneath the skin gathered languidly, relaxed. Boot waited for the light to change, to fill the room with the most sanguine colors, for the room to look as though it were some visceral chamber. The watch was an auburn glob, a round stain that could have been made by Mara and Boot.

Mara opened her eyes. The irises had taken on the crimson color of the room: she looked as though she wore contact lenses cut from red glass. Boot listened to the slight but persistent ticking, a diminished sound that pierced Mara's breathing, the rustling of clean sheets. Mara rocked on her hips, pushed against Boot split and wet flesh. Boot squeezed the watch, ran it along Mara's ribs, touched the underside of a breast with smooth metal. Mara looked at Boot and felt the chain and saw the watch and strained, opened her eyes, and said, "I'm glad you came to bed. What's that?"

She pointed at the watch.

Boot lay on his back. Mara curled against him. He let the watch swing in the last shadows: the room seemed to be slipping through the end of the spectrum. Walls and furniture took the blue cast of evening. Mara had the eyes of a hypnotist's subject.

"A present," said Boot. "Part of a dowry."

"Are you getting married?" said Mara.

"Do you want to get married?" said Boot.

"Don't make jokes," said Mara.

"It's a dead man's watch," said Boot. "An Englishman's watch. A dead Englishman who had the good luck to play cards in India."

Mara held the watch to her ear.

"It's ticking," she said.

Boot took it back and snapped it open and saw that one word was engraved in an elaborate script: *"Honour."*

Boot began to chuckle. He reached for the bottle of wine that Ulla had given him, opened it, and drank. The watch had been left on the bed: it made the sheets look like the soft fabric of a jeweler's display case.

"Something might happen," said Mara. "Please. Don't talk. I'm sore and I'm tired and I want to go to sleep."

"Good," said Boot.

To be sure. Something might happen.

He pulled on a pair of pants and took the wine and the watch and sat in the arbor where it was cool. There was one light on the hill, but not the least sound. Boot opened the watch every now and then to see the time, tried to calculate the amount of alcohol consumed by Ulla and her husband. He knew that Ulla sat on the bed and the old man sat on a stool and that they passed the jug between them. Ulla stared at the photograph of her wedding party (in which her husband proudly wore the watch). The ceramic jug was in a wicker basket. Her husband had no expression: his eyes were fixed on a wall that had become as yellow as old fingernails. Boot waited, looked at the watch, held it to starlight. *At least one jug is gone and that's a quart apiece, although Ulla is probably drinking more than her husband.*

Bugs filled the darkness. Boot looked at the quiet fields, the cove that now seemed as though it were filled with ink instead of water. There were no lights on the mainland or in the strait. Boot waited and looked at the watch and saw that it was a quarter to eleven. The lantern was still burning in Ulla's house.

At least two jugs are gone, two quarts for Ulla, and maybe a little more than that if she's drinking faster, taking more from the jug than the old man.

The watch swung back and forth. Boot waited, sipped the wine; it was a sharp retsina, one that tasted of pine trees. Boot went into the kitchen and took a piece of cold fish and bread and olives and an onion and ate them in the arbor. Boot had bought the fish from Petros and had cooked it over an open fire. The fish tasted of charcoal and the lemon and oil that covered it. Boot sliced the onion and ate it with the fish.

The first shout came from the house on the hill.

Boot cleared away the dishes, capped the jug of wine, and sat in the arbor. He smoked a cigarette, but held his hand over the end so no one could see the red point. The smoke drifted into the cool leaves above his head.

Boot finished the cigarette. *So two others are buying their way out, except this time the price is going to be a little higher, not just a jackass at fluctuating market values, but privacy, something appreciated more than anything else because it's so hard to come by, and memory, the residue of a man's and woman's youth, however pinched and mercenary.*

The watch seemed solvent and hazy in the light from the stars and moon, as though it weren't made from gold but spun from a soft and resilient fiber. Boot listened to the ticking. *I don't really want to do this. Ulla was generous to me when I first arrived, brought from her garden the most ripe and delicious vegetables, had been amazed when she saw a book. She called me professor because I could read. But word will get around and some people on this island will think twice before offering an insult.*

Boot started at the sound of wings in the dark air, a bird hunting over the fields. He lit another cigarette and drank wine.

He waited and listened and heard a pebble bouncing on the switchback that led to Ulla's house. He glanced through the leaves at the sky, which was as rich with stars as the sea with phosphorous.

"They're asleep," said Ulla.

The old man screamed.

Boot heard pebbles slithering down the side of the hill, Ulla's running footsteps, and then he knew she had fallen, because the sound of the footsteps stopped, replaced by the sound of a used body striking earth.

The old man shouted and threw stones.

Ulla was up and running again. She came down the path and through the arbor so quickly that Boot was startled: she left the stench of the labor in the fields, the quick wake of her own locomotion. Insects squawked on the hillside behind the house. Ulla was at the door, rattling the latch and the glass panes, shouting, clawing at the hinges. She struck the cracked wood and plaster at the side of the frame. Boot sat in the chair. Ulla remembered the key she had brought from her house and tried that, searched for the hole, but her haste and drunkenness made it impossible to find. She dropped the key and began to swear, uttered curses that called upon the memory of arguments so bitter as to require absolute privacy. So the key was gone and Ulla groped on the terrace in front of Boot's house, alternately moaning to herself and swearing. She gave up the search when she kicked the key: it rang twice on the stone terrace and then flew toward the fields. Ulla returned to the door and banged on the wood and glass. It had been both of them, husband and wife together, because it was his watch but her dowry, so they had to agree on the gift of the emblem of their strength. And that's where it hurt: the insult wasn't enough. For Ulla (and her husband as well) it was like loving an idiot child and finding that idiocy didn't stop maliciousness: the land, the uncomfortable years spent on it and alone in their house on the hill.

Ulla was clearly visible in the light from the stars and moon. Boot lit a cigarette. Ulla turned once and Boot saw that the water from her eyes had cut the dirt of a week's labor. She glanced at Boot but really didn't see, and said, "Go back up to the house."

"No," said Boot.

Ulla turned again and saw Boot.

"Here," said Boot.

Ulla moved quickly through the arbor. Boot dropped the watch into her cupped hands. She held it to the light, examined it carefully, appeared satisfied that it was still as defined as when her father took it from his trunk and offered it to her husband. Ulla rubbed the watch on her apron and held it in her hand and put the hand in a pocket.

"You should have thought of something better," said Boot.

"Don't go for the carnival," said Ulla. "Petros said . . ."

"No," said Boot. "That's not it."

Ulla held the watch and wiped her face on her apron.

"There wasn't anything better," said Ulla, letting the water run out of her eyes. She took the watch from the pocket, its chain was strung through her fingers like a rosary.

"I could tell you everything I hear," said Ulla.

"No," said Boot. "Just tell them you knocked on my door."

Ulla was hideously free: she was beyond the prospect of humiliation. Perhaps it had happened because the life necessary to work the land had taken too large a toll, or because there weren't enough memories to sustain, to be turned into the stuff of resistance. Perhaps, also, it was age. Ulla had lived too long and had not received in any fashion enough, so it was impossible for her to give Boot the watch and walk up the path to her house and eat the nightly fried egg, olives, and a piece of sausage and climb into bed where she would put her back to the old man and lie secure in the knowledge that nothing could break her and consequently something would break Boot.

"Here," said Boot, offering the jug. "Maybe you need a little."

"I'm going to be sick now," said Ulla as she turned and

leaned over the terrace and vomited, making the ancient sounds of liquidity and upheaval. She kneeled on the terrace, wiped her face with her apron, and smiled at Boot.

She shouldn't have done it there. That's where the key fell.

Ulla rocked back on her haunches, pushed herself up, and climbed the path to her house. Boot didn't hear a word from her husband.

Boot lit a lantern and put a rag around half of it and walked down into the field and searched through the plants and then found it in the round stain. He cleaned it with a rag, walked up the path to Ulla's house, and hung the key on a hook next to the door. He put out the lantern and went back to his house.

"What was that?" said Mara. She sat on the edge of the bed.

"Shhh," said Boot.

"She beat on the door," said Mara.

"Let's go to bed," said Boot.

"Jesus," said Mara.

"Shhh," said Boot. "Do you want some wine?"

He held up the jug.

"No," said Mara.

"Good," said Boot. He got into bed and pulled Mara next to him and went to sleep.

3
The Geek

The hoes worked in the fields. Boot woke to clear light, the pressure of warm and fragrant skin, the sight of the sheet wrapped so tightly around Mara's leg that it looked as though her calf and upper thigh had been cast in plaster. He felt a sleepy tenderness for her and he had a hangover that had been brewing for a week, so he woke her gently, bit and caressed ears, the nape of her neck, hips, buttocks, the backs of her thighs. The jackass brayed. The machinery of the well creaked. Boot touched the flat space behind Mara's ear with the tip of his tongue. Mara shook her head.

"Do you want to hear a crazy story?" said Boot.

"Leave me alone," said Mara.

"I'll tell the story," said Boot.

"No," said Mara. "It's not even six o'clock in the morning and I don't think I like getting up at this hour or any hour approaching it."

"We've got a boat to catch," said Boot.

131

"Oh," she said, turning and stretching, revealing herself before him. "What's the story?"

Boot said, "A friend, or anyway someone I knew a long time ago, was in love with an actress, a movie star, in love with her not because he had met her, but because he had seen all her films."

Mara yawned, bringing tears to her eyes. Boot listened to the hoes, looked at his clock. *We'll have just enough time.*

"So?" said Mara.

She sat with legs akimbo. One side of her face was marked by wrinkled cloth, sheet and pillowcase.

"So," said Boot, "I think he really felt something more than romantic claptrap about a movie actress. But he hadn't met her."

"Where are my clothes?" said Mara. "We've got a boat to catch. I'm awake now."

"No," said Boot, "there's time. I'll bring your clothes in. He was living in New York and he knew of a place where the actress went when she was in town. It's an expensive jet-set, bullshit kind of place. Anyway, this friend of mine saved his money, and when he heard the actress was in town, he'd rent evening clothes and go to the restaurant, hoping that she'd drop in. Which, of course, she did."

"Don't they have bodyguards or something?" said Mara.

"I guess so," said Boot, "but it really doesn't matter, because he would never have had the nerve or balls or whatever to say anything to her, so there wasn't any problem about that. No, he just sat and waited and watched her drink, knowing that there are certain absolute functions he could depend upon."

Mara smiled, posed, put his hand between her legs.

"We have time for this story," said Boot, "and that's about all. Maybe on the boat."

132

"I'd like that," said Mara.

"Good," said Boot. "We'll take a room." *If they haven't taken one for us already.* "There were things he could depend upon, and so he waited and the actress drank champagne and finally excused herself. And that's what he had been waiting for, because expensive or not, the restaurant only had one bathroom. She went downstairs and he waited, and then followed her as discreetly as he could, although he was trembling and shaking and looking like warmed-over shit in his rented clothes. So he went downstairs, too, and waited by the door. She breezed out, not even giving him a glance, but before she had even climbed two steps he had gone into the toilet, pulled down his pants, and sat on the seat."

Mara looked at the floor and shook her head.

"No," said Boot. "That's not it. You see, later he spent the last of his money and got so drunk I thought he was going to die. He came to me with his rented clothes stained and ripped and said, 'I wouldn't tell just anyone this, but Jesus, the seat was still warm.'"

Boot laughed and got out of bed and brought Mara her clothes. She looked at Boot and laughed as she dressed. Boot pulled on clothes and walked through the fields.

Boot watched the swinging hoes, the jackass turning in harness. *It's too bad about that extra season: Ulla won't see it. I wonder how she told Petros.*

Scorpions moved beneath the leaves. Boot stood before Ulla and her husband, but they didn't break stride or acknowledge his presence. Water that seemed as clear as liquid diamonds flowed in the channels between the plants. Ulla looked up once, glanced at the jackass and the sun, apparently trying to judge the amount of time that would have to pass before the heat made it impossible to continue. Boot saw the marks on her face: her eyes still ran as she worked. *That's how she told Petros. She just let him see the wet face, and maybe she held the watch for him to see, and that was all.*

Boot and Mara climbed the ridge. Mara looked over her shoulder and said, "It's a pretty house. And the bay."

The opium smuggler was still in his yard, having spent the previous afternoon and night in the same position, or nearly in the same position, stirring only when muscles cramped or when he had to find something to drink, but he always returned to the comfortable roots of the tree. His dog sat next to him. The leaves of the tree undulated softly. The opium smuggler smoked a cigarette.

"It wasn't much of a watch," said the opium smuggler.

"You'd be surprised," said Boot.

The opium smuggler smiled.

"Maybe I would, and maybe a lot of people have been," said the opium smuggler. "But you should remember she's just an old woman."

"And her husband," said Boot.

"Can you tell them apart?" said the opium smuggler.

"She's got more backbone," said Boot.

The opium smuggler laughed and slapped his dog. Dust rose from the black fur.

"Yes," said the opium smuggler.

"So," said Boot, "I've paid for the time and the animal and more."

The opium smuggler shrugged. He looked for ticks in the dog's fur, found one, and held the tip of his cigarette next to it. Black fur burned. The tick moved. The opium smuggler caught the tick between his thumbs and rolled the nails together. Boot heard a slight crack. The opium smuggler wiped his hands on the dog's fur.

"So," said Boot, "maybe you should talk to Ulla, and maybe now they'll grow opium, and then she can get a better watch."

The opium smuggler's gestures were carefully made: a raised brow, a sharp eye, a puff of smoke. There wasn't the least sign of expectation.

"Because the land isn't much good to her now," said Boot.

The opium smuggler glanced at Boot.

There isn't a politician in the world who wouldn't give both legs for that look.

The opium smuggler said, "Jesus Christ, I was wrong. Maybe people should be surprised."

"Yes," said Boot. "Maybe."

"Thanks," said the opium smuggler.

"Wait," said Boot. "Isn't there something else?"

The opium smuggler looked at the dog, stared across the strait, and said, "Sure I'll do you a favor. I'll just tell them to watch out."

"Good," said Boot. *He can't tell them more, can't let anyone know that opium is going to be grown here on the island.* "That'll be enough. Especially if you don't tell them why. That's the best part."

Boot smiled.

"And of course . . ." said the opium smuggler.

"No," said Boot. "For the same reason that you can't tell them why, either. I don't want them to know."

The opium smuggler laughed, shook his head, and kicked his dog. He stood and began to walk along the ridge, toward the fields in front of Boot's house. The dog followed, jumping and wagging its tail.

In the car Boot turned on the radio.

"Turn that down," said Mara. "What's going on?"

135

"Nothing," said Boot. *Petros must have stopped on his way in, with his catch, because that's about the time Ulla gets up, so he stopped and looked and maybe even heard something and went to the market, and that usually closes about seven. And now he should be on his way back, because one look at Ulla wouldn't have been enough.*

"What time is it?" said Boot.

"A little before seven," said Mara.

"Pull over," said Boot. "Someplace where we can look at the sea."

"I thought we didn't have the time," said Mara.

"We have the time for this," said Boot. "Pull over."

Boot stood at the edge of the precipice. The sea was so clear that the bottom looked like a relief map. The sun was up and the blue predawn sky was shattered by light.

"What are we waiting for?" said Mara.

"What?" said Boot, but then he knew he had been wrong. Petros' stupidity had made it necessary for another look at Ulla.

So Boot leaned against the fender of the car and saw on the road from town a trail of dust that was so thick and so obviously coming from one moving source that it seemed to be smoke from a locomotive rather than dust; the Renault (which was rusted to the point of looking as though it were alive and covered with a skin condition of serious proportions) came up the road from the monastery, and it wasn't moving just fast, but at a rate far beyond haste or danger. Boot heard the banging of pots and pans, knives and forks, the rolls of barbed wire, the shifting of the peddler's load. Thymos bounced, hit his head on the ceiling of the Renault, didn't bother to look at Mara or Boot or the red car or anything, being solely intent on keeping the station wagon on the road.

Boot got into the car and said, "Drive slowly."

It will take at least ten minutes even if Thymos jumps from the Renault and runs to the fields where Ulla, the old man, and the opium smuggler will be talking. And the opium smuggler won't want Thymos around long, either, so he'll just look at him once (if you can call what the opium smuggler does with his eyes looking) and say, Be careful.

"This is going to ruin my car," said Mara.

"We'll get a jackass," said Boot.

"Sure," said Mara.

They could see the ship from the edge of town. It was an old one with a single smokestack, a ship that had been making the circuit between the islands for some time, originally as luxurious transportation for well-to-do foreigners (it was still possible to see fine woodwork and brass fittings), but now there were few first-class cabins, and the rest of the ship had been made over to resemble others that traveled between the islands. A large space had been cleared on the main deck to accommodate passengers, goats, chickens, jackasses, dogs. A passenger sat on his suitcases and held his lunch in a piece of cloth. The open space on the deck was also filled with crates, goods that were shipped from one island to another. The crates were lashed to the deck because most of the routes were short and the freight had to be easily accessible. On the covered interior part of the main deck there were some benches made of slats. In peak travel times the entire space was filled, seats and deck alike. It was not very comfortable during rough weather, since most people and even some of the animals became sick, and the passengers sat in their own filth, silently praying for the rough weather and the journey to end.

On the quay at the side of the ship there were barriers, people standing nervously behind them, attempting, as much as space permitted, to keep away from one another. Between the barriers and the ship cranes moved, lifted crates to the deck, a cargo of produce, hoes and shovels, primitive farm equipment, a new pump with a gasoline engine, boxes marked with red crosses. There wasn't that much freight. The route was limited to three islands, Samos, Ikaria, and one other: they seemed to be a natural collection only because there was so much distance between them and the next islands, and so they were quarantined together, perhaps because each island wasn't entirely sufficient unto itself. The three were geared together in comfortable symbiosis.

Mara looked at the ship, necessity grafted to elegance, the sides stained by the steady flow of bilge. She had the expression of one who is inspecting a newly purchased plot in a cemetery.

"They don't sink," said Boot. "Don't look so worried."

"It's not the ship," said Mara.

Boot stood in the sunlight.

"Look," said Mara, "all I want is a room."

Boot walked to the ticket window of the steamship line and said, "What's the difference between these and two round-trip tickets in a room, first class?"

Boot looked over his shoulder and saw Costas, Pavlos, Petros, and Giorgos.

"They've been paid for," said the clerk. He spoke without moving his lips, as though he were some pale and sequestered showman: the sound seemed to come not from his face or body, but from the ticket seller's box alone. "Here."

Boot stuck his tickets under the bars and took the new envelope and turned to Costas, Pavlos, Petros, and Giorgos and said, "I think the watch was worth more than that."

"She's just an old woman," said Pavlos. "Old and worn out."

"You should be so old and worn out," said Boot.

"Spunky today," said Costas.

"Here," said Pavlos. He gave Boot a bag with two bottles of ouzo in it. "For the trip."

"Thanks," said Boot.

"At your command," said Pavlos, using the ancient phrase that still survived in the language, the linguistic correlative of the ruins at the other end of the island.

Boot smiled. The four of them gazed at him with blank expressions. Boot waited for Thymos, for the message: because then they'd have one day and one night to haggle over and be frightened by the fact that the one person on the island with whom they would never trade, with whom they would not even begin to think of trading (since they knew they would have about the same chances as the English officer in the card game), had given them a definite warning to be careful or they'd find themselves on the short end of the bargain.

The five of them stood amid the sounds of the port, rattling chains, creaking blocks, the dripping of bilge from the side of the ship.

At the end of the quay there were two men who were isolated from the other passengers. One was counting money and small slips of paper. The other held two chickens. The man with the chickens took half the money and a slip of paper and gave the first man the chickens and then began to mingle with the other passengers. He had put the slip of paper in his shirt pocket and the money in his wallet. The people behind the barrier avoided him: he had already been drinking wine, and he was dirty and he stank and when he spoke he slurred. He had lost his teeth, too, except for one black stump. The passengers were afraid of contagion and they were suspicious of the man because he wasn't from Samos.

The other man, the one who had been counting money and who now had the chickens, stood at the end of the quay and watched the passengers. He had pomade on his hair and a waxed mustache and large eyes, but his coat was dirty and his tie stained and his pants were held up by a piece of rope. He just stood in the shadow of the ship and seemed pleased as the man with the stump moved farther into the crowd.

Boot looked at the man with the black stump and the man with the chickens and said to Costas, "Are they doing business?"

Costas shrugged.

"Looks like a lottery," said Boot.

Costas had the sharpest hearing, so he heard it first, the sound of the Renault's engine cranked up to the point of obvious danger, if not for Thymos, then for his livelihood: the cost of repairing a thrown rod would bring Thymos to bankruptcy. So Costas heard it and looked at Boot and then at the others. Boot saw Costas' expression and smiled and then he heard it, too. The smile hardened, turned into a grimace, and Pavlos, Giorgos, and Petros heard the sound, looked at Boot, and excused themselves. They walked to the curb and stood next to the rusted Renault.

"Come on," said Boot. "We've got a room."

"And what's that?" said Mara.

"Liquor," said Boot.

He took her by the hand and led her through the heat to the barrier, where he greeted the passengers he recognized, joked with the stevedores in blue shirts and white pants, pushed through worn hand luggage, goats, pigs, and dogs, and found a place in the shade for Mara to sit down.

"It's hot," said Mara.

The man who had the slip of paper in his pocket, the one who was circulating among the passengers, came over to Boot and said, "You're bringing the carnival."

"Yes," said Boot. "What were you doing with the chickens?"

"Chickens?" said the man with one black stump in his mouth. "I haven't seen any chickens."

"What's this?" said Boot, picking a feather from the man's sleeve. The coat was spliced together, a collection of grafts from the ragpicker: the sleeves didn't match and the buttons didn't fit into their holes.

Mara stared at the man with the black stump, the face that looked like a brown paper sack. Boot held the feather. People shuffled in their festive clothes: traveling, even to a neighboring island, was something of a luxury, a cause for celebration. Mara listened to the bleating animals, heard a shout from the bridge of the ship. A stevedore was struck by the hook at the end of a free line, and he shouted and swore, but he was more angry than hurt.

Mara was compelled by the growing distance between herself and the bleating animals, the ship that seemed to be bleeding rust and water, the booms and cranes etched on blue sky. The man with the stump looked at Mara, but she was beyond noticing: in the midst of that oozing aloofness she had been struck by the fact of being alive.

Boot held the feather.

"A chicken feather," said the man with the black stump. "Be sure you bring the geek."

Mara looked at the feather and slipped away. She had acidly cherished regret. Now it had been turned into desire, and if desire were satisfied she'd be left with the terrifying vision of no one.

"I'll bring the carnival," said Boot.

"You do that," said the man. He smiled his stump and moved farther down the quay.

"We need a carnival," said an old woman with a goat.

"Jesus," said Boot. Mara drank from one of the new bottles. "You're picking up my worst habits. At least you could use a glass."

"No," said Mara. "This way you get just as much as you want. Can we go to our room?"

"Wait," said Boot.

The old woman milked the goat: at each tug her fingers spread like an Indian dancer's. The milk hissed in the bottom of a tin cup. The woman tasted the milk and then gave a sip to a child who was sitting next to the goat.

Costas, Pavlos, Petros, and Giorgos stood next to the Renault. Thymos spoke, knocked the dust from his clothes, slammed the door of the station wagon: his wares looked like those in the store after it had been invaded by the jackass. Water ran from the Renault, made a sound like a cow urinating on a stone. Steam drifted from the grille. Then all of them, the peddler included, walked from the curb to the quay.

"They don't look cheerful," said Mara.

Costas and the rest pushed through the crowd and stood before Boot.

"So," said Boot, "how much is the watch worth now?"

The five of them stood at the side of the ship, next to the dripping bilge. Each had the expression of a swimmer who'd just seen the fin of a shark.

"I'll bring the carnival," said Boot.

Boot took Mara by the hand and began to walk to the

gangplank. It was gray and chipped, and the runglike slats that had helped passengers keep their footing were a worn reminder to take care. The man with the black stump and the woman with the goat were already showing their tickets to a member of the crew.

"Wait," said Costas.

Boot turned.

"What was it?" said Costas.

Boot said, "Ask the opium smuggler."

"Maybe we can work something out," said Costas.

"No way," said Boot.

He stepped onto the gangplank.

"What's the price of a jackass?" said Costas.

Boot shook his head. Costas approached hesitantly.

"It wasn't the jackass," said Boot.

"Jesus Christ," said Petros. "What was it?"

"Shut up," said Costas.

"Come on," said Boot. He took Mara's hand and led her up the gangplank and onto the ship. They walked to the upper deck and were given the key to their room.

"Let's get undressed," said Mara.

"In a minute," said Boot.

Boot touched the old wood and the brass fittings as they walked through the halls to the deck. Propellers turned: the water looked as though it were being mixed with milk as the sand was brought up from the harbor floor. Costas, Pavlos, and Petros stood and watched as the lines were cast off. Mara drank. Boot stood at the rail and stared at the water until it was the color of blue ink. It was impossible to resolve the quay, the people standing on it; even the town itself was drawn together, appearing to be no more than a whitish deposit above the water. The island seemed to slide away: Boot saw all of one side, the scrubby vegetation on land that seemed antithetical to any creature requiring food and shelter, the white speck of the monastery, and, at the end of the island, the colony of lepers.

"Have you seen them?" said Boot.

"What?" said Mara.

"The lepers," said Boot.

"No," said Mara. "Let's go to our room."

The engine labored below deck. Every piece of tin rattled. Guy wires trembled. Inside the narrow berth Boot pushed Mara's side and buttocks against the wooden wall and moved inside her, held her so she could feel the vibration in the wood. They lay face to face. She bit him and pulled his hair and shook her head, moved away from him, held his penis between her legs, ran it along the inside of her thighs, across her stomach, under a breast, in the hollow of her neck, finally held him in her mouth and then stopped and caressed him with a handful of her hair while kissing and sucking his testicles. Boot touched the trembling wall, her flesh. She settled over him, dragged a nipple across his lips. There were sounds from the ship: shuffling feet, the thumping of the loose machinery below the deck, angry voices, quarrels over spots near the rail, the bleating of goats, the squawking of chickens, the braying of a jackass. Mara licked the perspiration from Boot's chest.

"I want it on the floor," said Mara, "like a dog."

She kneeled on the deck and Boot covered her, watched the muscles working in her thighs, the contraction of buttocks, hair spread over the skin of her back. Boot felt the throbbing of the deck in his knees. There was the farting sound of trapped air. Boot pulled her against his thighs, scratched her head, bit through moving skin her ribs and spine, saw the white spots left by his thumbs and fingers. The veins of Mara's arms were corded, distinct: her hands were spread over the seams of the deck. They lay in the berth, side by side, joined: a thin line of saliva fell from the corner of Mara's mouth, but she watched Boot's face, waited for and then saw the squint and start, the marked expression. They listened to vibrating wires and tin, the locomotive pounding from the engine room, the arguments about space and animals.

"Did anyone look in the window?" said Mara.

"I wasn't watching," said Boot. "It's a porthole, not a window."

"Whatever," said Mara. "People can look through it, can't they?"

"Yes," said Boot.

Mara sat up, reached for the bottle, and drank.

"This thing doesn't sound like a ship," said Boot. "It sounds like a marching band."

"Want some?" said Mara.

"Yes," said Boot. "What if there's a child?"

"I'd have an abortion," said Mara.

"You keep the bottle," said Boot.

He pulled on his clothes and went into the corridor, walked across a green rug that had been at one time deep and luxurious but was now thin, marked by two paths; it looked as though a dogcart had been run up and down the halls. Boot glanced at the bored barmen in the first-class lounge and shook his head and then walked down to the main deck.

"Yes," said Boot. "I'm going to bring the carnival."

Islanders smiled. Boot moved amid the luggage, the uneasy animals. People mingled freely now: they thought the sea air proof against disease, and the passengers felt the camaraderie of pilgrims. It was good for business, since the minute the man with the stump and his associate (actually brother) felt free to walk among the passengers they began. The business (fraud or racket would be more accurate) worked like this: The man with the black stump and his brother, a man who was more slender but equally filthy, although more convincing and sly and spirited, too, boarded a ship. The sly and older brother carried two chickens, a fistful of tickets, and a brown paper sack. The tickets were paired. When the passengers had settled into the monotony of the heat and pounding engines, the sly brother held up the birds and announced in no humble fashion that there was to be a lottery, the prize of which would be the two specimens of the barnyard. Then he proceeded to cajole and humiliate the passengers into buying a ticket. Each ticket cost a little less than a nickel. One of the paired tickets was kept by the unfortunate gambler-purchaser (sucker is what the sly one called them) and the other went into the brown sack. The man with the stump was, at this point, desperately denying any connection with the pitchman, the hustler, but he helped the act by fingering the goods, praising the birds (which were sorely in need of it, especially if compliments could give them meat and an even covering of feathers and animation that could be mistaken for life), fingering thighs and legs, and pantomiming the plucking, gutting, cooking, and eating of the chickens. The man with the stump went so far as to buy a ticket. It immediately went into his pocket and was exchanged for another that he had received earlier, the other half of which was already palmed by the organizer of the raffle. When the last penny had been squeezed out of the suckers (it's an accurate word, because if they couldn't see what was going on, then in fact they were), the sly one, the brother with the broad, easy voice and cutting wit, held up the brown paper sack, shook it, walked up and down the deck, wished each buyer luck, praised the beauty of plain women, estimated the take to within a dime, pulled the palmed ticket from the bag, and said, "Here! Here! This is the ticket that will bring the lucky owner the pleasure of devouring not one, but two entire chickens!" He gave the number and the man with the stump blushed and shouted and danced like a fool through the crowds, looking not so much pleased that he had actually won two chickens and a lottery on top of it, but a little ill at ease and angry that he was going to have to hold two chickens by their feet for the rest of the voyage. The organizer of the raffle collected the losing tickets. The short distances between the islands gave the man with the stump some consolation.

When the ship was at its moorings, the man with the stump met more or less secretly with his sly brother and the ticket was exchanged for the birds and the take was split and they waited for passengers to come on board so the process could begin again, which it did until there was a break in the routine: when the chickens were dead, or just about dead, or when the difference between the two conditions was so slight as to be purely academic (and the brothers had some fairly heated conversation about precisely when this particular condition occurred), the birds were in fact raffled off, and the brothers left the ship and found a farmer who would be willing to part with two chickens at a reasonable price.

These birds, the ones that Boot watched as they were circulated on the open deck, had experienced more than what even the sly brother considered a fair number of raffles. Business was bad: the route was limited.

"Pretty nice birds," said the man with the face like a bag and the mouth marked by the black stump.

"Yes," said Boot. "I can see they're good birds."

"Tasty, I'll bet," said the man.

"How can you eat a chicken if you only have one tooth?" said Boot.

"Stew it and mash it and eat it with a piece of bread dipped in the pulp," said the man. "Here."

He offered a ticket.

"What's this?" said Boot.

"It's a ticket," said the man. "For the raffle."

"I didn't see you buy it," said Boot.

"Shit," said the man with one tooth. "Who are you kidding? I need a drink."

Boot watched the brother work with the chickens: he accosted the woman with the goat and child, felt the thinness of the girl's limbs, accurately judged her health.

"But the price of a drink is three times the price of the ticket," said Boot.

"Who are you kidding?" said the man.

The brother's fondling of the girl was so close to an insult as to look like part of the pitch: forcing the woman with the goat to buy a ticket because she was ashamed of her daughter's health, or just to keep the brother's filthy hands away from the child.

"No one," said Boot. "Go away."

"Come on," said the younger brother. There was the saw edge of pleading in his voice. "Take it."

"Here," said Boot, giving him the price of a drink. "Have a drink. I don't want the ticket."

"I don't want the charity," said the man.

He slipped the ticket into Boot's shirt pocket and disappeared with the grace of a small-time pickpocket. The man with the chickens was talking the last of the most stubborn passengers into buying a ticket. At the rail next to Boot there was an old islander, a man dressed in the ceremonial uniform of his village: black baggy trousers, a white shirt with billowing sleeves, a red sash at the waist, and a skullcap. The man sat on a plastic suitcase. The ship labored in choppy straits. Bits of shattered rainbow, light in windblown mist, appeared along the railing.

"Do you want a ticket?" said Boot.

"Not in this lottery," said the man on the plastic suitcase. "It's a waste of money."

"Half price," said Boot.

"No," said the man. He sat in rigid profile, his arms akimbo, as proud as only a man can be wearing the outdated but somehow strident uniform (if not the same cloth) that his great-grandfather had worn to fight the Turks.

The man with the stump drank from a bottle.

"It's a winner," said Boot.

"Sure," said the man in the skullcap. "You keep it."

Someone said, "Draw it."

The man with the chickens reached into the bag and produced the palmed ticket.

"What is it?" said the woman with the goat.

The man with the chickens gave the number and everyone who had bought a ticket sighed and shrugged their shoulders. Boot leaned against the railing, watched the sea slide by. The man with the chickens said, "You have a ticket, don't you?"

"Yes," said Boot.

He took it from his pocket.

"The winning number," said the man with the chickens. "You see, he's ashamed of his good fortune."

Boot took the birds.

"Thanks," said Boot.

"No need to thank me," said the man. "Thank the Lord for a full stomach."

149

Goddamn, why didn't I just throw the fucking ticket over-board, because at least I could have done that, but you can't throw two chickens overboard, certainly not in front of hun-gry people who won't take charity.

"Can I have the ticket?" said the organizer of the raffle.

"Sure," said Boot.

The birds squawked; their feet were tied together with a piece of twine. Boot handed the ticket over and knew that even throwing the ticket into the sea wouldn't have done any good, since there were already two tickets with the same number in the sly brother's hand, which meant that there had been three altogether. So even if Boot had said, No, I don't have a ticket, the brother would have reached into Boot's pocket and come up with two paired tickets and Boot would have been given the birds.

The man in the uniform (or costume: time was blurring the distinction) looked at the birds and said, "I don't under-stand. They're still alive."

"You should have bought the ticket," said Boot.

"Yes," said the man.

"Would you like to buy two chickens?" said Boot.

"I had the money for the ticket," said the man. "Not for the birds."

Boot shrugged and walked among the passengers, worked his way between animals and suitcases, and stopped in front of a woman who had chickens and feed, a coffee can filled with grain. He bought a handful and walked to the rail and said to the younger brother, the man with the black stump, "Did Costas pay you well?"

"More than the price of two birds," said the man with the stump.

"I'm sure," said Boot.

"They're still alive," said the man with the stump.

Boot watched him drink, looked for a moment at the sea, capped and blue, water that looked like painted and lacquered metal.

"Sometimes just before they're dead," said the man with the stump, "no one buys a ticket."

Boot held the birds over his hand; two beaks pecked at the heel of his palm.

"So," said Boot.

"Well," said the man with the stump, "my brother takes them into an empty room, puts the head in a drawer, and fucks the bird, because if an egg can come out . . . Anyway, he fucks them and when he comes he slams the drawer shut and that makes the bird grab. He says there's nothing like it."

The muscles in the man's face tightened. Boot realized he was grinning.

"Then what?" said Boot. "Does he leave the chickens there, in the drawer?"

"No," said the man with the stump. "He does it twice, once to each bird, and then puts them in a sack and waits until we get off the ship so he can throw them away. He calls them darling and sweetheart when they're in the drawer."

Tin rattled. Guy wires hummed. Boot could smell the rank odor of petroleum from the smokestack.

"How about you?" said Boot. "You tried it?"

The man with the stump held the bottle halfway between the rail and his mouth.

"If he had let me I wouldn't have told you. I'm surprised. They told me you were sharp."

"Not always," said Boot. "Look, I have two chickens."

The man with the stump seemed protected and closed: his face lapsed into blank indifference.

"Give them to the geek," he said. "He'll take them."

Boot went into the first-class lounge and asked for a drink and a glass of water. The barman looked at the chickens, the handful of grain on the bar, Boot untying the twine that held the scaled legs together. The birds trembled. Boot put them on the floor along with the glass of water and a little grain. The birds ate. Boot drank. The barman looked at Boot's face once and didn't say a word about the shitting chickens.

"I guess they won't have a drink," said Boot. "Ouzo."

"No," said the barman.

"I'll have one," said Boot, pushing the empty glass across the bar.

Boot held each bird with its beak at the crack between two planks in the deck, waited for a moment, and withdrew his hands with a bombmaker's gentleness. The chickens stared at the crack, remained motionless, became hypnotized.

The repetitious sounds of the ship's locomotion filled the lounge.

"Why should you win them?" said the woman with the goat.

She stood just beyond the threshold, obviously appalled at the prospect of stepping into a chamber of her natural enemies: those who had the time, taste, and money for luxury.

"It was fixed," said Boot. "It's always fixed."

The woman gave the interior of the lounge one angry glance, said, "Isn't that the truth," and led her goat away.

Boot held the scaled and spikelike feet, took the grain from the bar, and walked through the corridor to his room. Mara was still sitting in the berth.

"Don't ask," said Boot.

"What do you mean?" said Mara. "What are you doing with those chickens?"

"That's what I meant."

Boot looked at the stained sheets, the drying mark that had the shape of the opening of a woman's genitals.

"I'm tired," said Boot. "I won a raffle. These birds are the prize."

Boot stood in front of the berth with the two birds and a handful of grain. There was the sting of hysteria in Mara's laughter. Boot put the birds in the closet and threw the grain in with them and closed the door.

"Try to sleep," said Boot. "We'll be there soon. An hour maybe."

"Wash your hands," said Mara.

She stood next to him at the sink, picking the chicken feathers from his shirt and pants.

"Christ," said Boot.

Boot and Mara sat opposite each other on the berth. The chickens moved in the closet. Mara stared out the porthole, obviously wishing she were somewhere or somebody else, but knowing she could be neither; so every now and then she scowled at Boot, and he smiled and kissed her and then looked out the porthole, too. Small islands, really nothing more than bits of rock, revolved around the ship: they gave the sea a reassuring aspect, a sense of intimacy and small-ness, the feeling that it could be both known and managed.

"Don't look at me," said Mara.

The room was filled with the fertile sound of water cut by the prow, a skeletal creaking of timber.

"You're vain and vulgar and disgusting," said Mara. "And why did you bring those birds in here?"

Boot laughed and said, "Because I couldn't throw them overboard."

153

Mara pulled the sheet over her shoulder and turned her back to Boot and said, "At least you could wring their necks. That way I wouldn't have to listen to them rustling in the closet."

"You could do it," said Boot. "After all, I went to the trouble of winning them."

The sheet was sculpted by Mara's body: blond hair curled over white stone. The cloth was drawn and ridged by her fist. Boot saw that the bottle was almost empty and then felt bad for baiting her.

Mara jumped from the berth, opened the closet door, and said, "Shit." She grabbed a bird, first by a wing and then by the head, and began to swing the body.

"No," said Boot. "I'll need them."

The bird flapped its wings, reached with splayed feet for Mara's legs.

"I'm sorry," said Boot.

Mara put the bird back in the closet, slammed the door, and said, "Shit." There was a feather on the inside of her thigh. She washed her hands and climbed into bed and was asleep before the birds had time to get reacquainted with the darkness. Boot picked the feather from her skin.

Through the porthole Boot could see horizon, water, and sky blended together. Mara slept nude. Boot was confused by her presence, so awed by the mystery of flesh that he felt the constricted and appalling tug of God.

The carnival was on Ikaria (namesake of Icarus, headstone of his final descent), which was known for two reasons, the first being the beauty of its women, which was not only legendary (any islander would say that beautiful wives came from Ikaria), but fact as well: Boot had been to the island once before, when he was first traveling to Samos, and at the docking of the ship he had been stunned by the sight of a quay on which there stood and sat beautiful women of all ages. The younger ones had worn school uniforms, but they seemed uncomfortable in them, as though their precocious womanliness was so apparent to each that the symbol of girlishness, the blue uniform, was a restriction on the obvious fact of maturity. And there seemed to be frustration even in the cut and color of the dresses: the uniforms were institutionally grim, but they enhanced deeply colored skin, dark eyes and hair, white teeth. The older women were striking as well, although hardened by labor in the fields, birth, drunken husbands, and drink itself, but even in the figures of those who seemed most abused there was a taut beauty. Boot had brought a drink to the rail and a girl who sold fruit on the quay smiled at him in a manner so naturally joyful and seductive that he seriously considered going to his room and packing his things. He tossed her a coin and she reached into her bag, found a small orange, and pitched it up to the rail: Boot scarcely had to move his hand. The girl lingered for a moment, put the coin in her pocket, and moved farther down the quay, looking once over her shoulder. Boot went back to his room after the ship had left its moorings and ate the orange and thought of the girl. The orange was small, sharp, and succulent.

Ikaria was also known for the quality of its wines.

Boot felt the dull bump and uneven roll of the ship as it reached the quay.

"Wake up," said Boot. "We're here."

"Oh," said Mara, "I feel sick."

Boot shrugged.

"We've got to find the carnival," said Boot. "Put your clothes on."

Mara dressed and Boot took the chickens from the closet and they walked to the gangplank.

"Christ," said Mara.

"Yes," said Boot. "They're beautiful."

It seemed as though Boot plucked an orange from the noisy air. A girl in a blue uniform waved and smiled and Boot searched for a coin, but the girl smiled again and shook her head. She was surrounded by goats, pigs, and chickens, swinging and netted freight, passengers carrying hand luggage, or things that resembled hand luggage, usually homemade boxes with leather hinges, or cardboard boxes, or just rags, bundles. The girl smiled and was gone, made invisible by the clutter of people, objects, and animals.

"You know her," said Mara.

"No," said Boot.

"Too bad," said Mara.

Boot put the orange into the bag with the bottles of liquor and picked up his chickens and walked onto the quay. The noise and the afternoon heat only complicated Mara's hangover. She took Boot's arm, shielded her eyes from the sun, swore in a gentle voice. Boot found a place for her in the shade and walked to the end of the quay.

"Where's the carnival?" said Boot.

The fisherman looked at the chickens and said, "You mean Vaggelis and the thieves?"

"I guess that's who I mean," said Boot.

"Do you have a guarantee?" said the fisherman.

Boot nodded.

"To test the geek?" said the fisherman. He gestured to the birds.

Boot said, "Where are they?"

The fisherman was talkative, perhaps because he was old and had seen a lot, or simply because he thought his years

156

had given him license to break the silence with the same things he would have said forty years earlier. Or maybe it was just the carnival, the experience of having it on the island for so long.

"It's a good thing," said the fisherman, "because since they arrived our women have been seduced, and if something isn't buried or hidden, it's stolen. And we can't get locks. We never needed locks before. Anyone can walk into my house."

"The women are beautiful," said Boot.

"Yes," said the fisherman. "It's a crime."

Because so much promise, which is the nature of beauty, should be cast on such barren rocks. Is that what makes it a crime? Or is it just the seduction?

"They're in a vacant lot," said the fisherman, "at the end of town. They're money grubbers. Hell is paved with gold."

The fisherman pointed a crooked finger toward the place: the knuckles looked like small walnuts.

"Just get them out of here," said the fisherman.

"At your command," said Boot.

He walked back to Mara.

"The name's Vaggelis," said Boot.

"I should have left you alone," said Mara. "Only I could get involved with somebody who chases jackasses all night."

Mara sat in the shade and felt the jarring chemistry of a hangover: irritated nerves only added to sexual need, the poverty of an untouched body.

"Let's go to a hotel where we can have some frenzy," said Mara.

"That's better," said Boot.

"I'm acting like a slut," said Mara.

"No," said Boot, "that's not true. I don't pay you."

Boot saw the lot. There were three canvas tents, and they

had been patched so many times they looked like shelters made from quilts: everything had been used, denim, nylon, bright pieces of what looked to be a parachute, sheets, stained silk, underwear still defined by yellowed lace. A goat was tied to a line. There were some benches and boxes, and a pot hung from three metal legs. Something was cooking in the pot and it smelled of garlic and onions. There were wagons near the tents, and they were filled with wood and poles and neatly rolled guy wires. The wagons were covered with black tarps. There were piles of trash around the tents, old posters, empty bottles and cans, newspapers and garbage. Two children and a dog were picking through the pile.

Vaggelis' carnival had eight members. There was a strongman who doubled as a freak. His body was covered with obscene tattoos, so when he wasn't bending bars over his head or twisting nails with his teeth, he was exhibited in a tent where only men were allowed. The acrobat was a cheerful thief. He had brought to the carnival a pampered German shepherd and had played a joke on Vaggelis. Vaggelis slaughtered the German shepherd, made a stew of the meat, and fed it to the acrobat. When the meal was finished, Vaggelis said, Your dog was in the stew. Two weeks later, on the mainland, Vaggelis gave the acrobat a mongrel puppy and said, I don't like jokes. The puppy grew into a dog that was even larger than the German shepherd. Its eyes were different colors and its fur looked as though it had been used as a mop. The completed bondage pleased Vaggelis: the dog and the acrobat were inseparable. The high-wire man was quiet. He was most happy when performing, when he could feel the shouts of the crowd, the laughter, and songs humming in the wire. There was a magician who knew the usual tricks and some other stunts, too, vulgar parodies of orthodoxy: a scrap of bread turned into meat, wine tricked into blood. These were popular among those whose beliefs were as strong as the magician's legerdemain was sleazy, whose faith was compounded of superstition and insanity. Occasionally one would have a seizure. The magician doubled as a pickpocket, and Vaggelis received a cut of whatever was dredged from the pockets of those in epileptic rapture. The palm reader doubled as a whore. She gave advice in a tent that was embroidered with gold thread, and she had a reputation, which was passed from man to man in the utmost secrecy, for curing impotence. The cure consisted mainly in the belief that she had a cure and a trick she had learned years before in a respectable whorehouse. The trick was holding a piece of ice against the back of a man's testicles. Vaggelis received a cut of her take. There was a man who couldn't speak: a congenital emptiness showed in his throat. He was terrified of bugs, and his name was Theodros. He did the cooking and cleaning, passed the hat, broke and set up camp, carried the heaviest trunks. Theodros was something of a doctor. With the thread and needle that were used to mend clothes he stitched the wounds of those who returned from town after a fight. The carnival had a geek, too.

Vaggelis served as ringmaster and general manager. He enticed people into the tent of the palm reader, praised the daring of the high-wire man, the skill of the acrobat, the muscles of the strongman, the humiliation of the geek. Vaggelis was one who believed that for every broken man in the world there was one less problem. He probed for weakness that could be ripped into cash, or if not cash, then amusement or safety. Vaggelis was a man who loved gossip.

This particular morning Vaggelis was uneasy. As far as he was concerned there were three or possibly four men in the world who understood anything near what he understood about money, and this was no mere vanity, either, since Vaggelis was rich, having deposited over the years tens of thousands in various bank accounts, the books for which he kept in a leather sack that was sewn to the bottom of one of his trunks. He wasn't really concerned that the acrobat and the magician were stealing the countryside blind, nor did he care about the number of women and girls who had been seduced: it was expected. Such behavior provided as much catharsis as the carnival itself, but even Vaggelis knew that the limits of vicarious sinning had been reached. He was waiting for a guarantee and would wait for it no matter how outraged the islanders became, because traveling without it would be as inconceivable as hell without fire: it was simply bad business, and soon every island would be reneging on pledges.

It wasn't the business of the carnival that bothered Vaggelis, but another, one that had provided the greater portion of the tens of thousands in his bank accounts, and this other business had to do with the fact that he was discreet and knew gossip and consequently had struck up a working relationship with an opium smuggler on Samos. And he really hadn't felt uneasy about opium until the palm reader approached his tent with the gray paper of a telegram. He understood figures but not letters; the knowledge that he would have to ask what it said was enough to put him in a foul mood for a week. The advisor gave the telegram to Vaggelis, and he opened it and stared at it and said, Christ, do I have to ask? The advisor took the gray paper and read, "Cooperate. Good business." The message was followed by the opium smuggler's name. So the uneasiness came from the fact that if there were three men in the world whom Vaggelis respected in monetary matters, and if he was the first, and a man who could be described as "in business" in Istanbul was the second, then the opium smuggler was the third. Vaggelis had heard gossip about the man who would be bringing the guarantee and had enjoyed the prospect of prodding him a little. But Vaggelis was alarmed because one man (and a foreigner at that) had been able to produce the telegram, a method of communication that in itself was still mythic in this part of the world. So Vaggelis knew that a great deal of money was involved, and his ignorance of the precise terms of the arrangement made him doubly uneasy, especially when he considered the sums deposited in various bank accounts.

So Vaggelis sat near the entrance of his tent, looking at a stool on which the gray scrap of paper had been left by the palm reader. And when he could no longer tolerate his thoughts he went outside and threw stones at the dogs and children who were digging through the garbage around the carnival tents, berated the acrobat and magician (although not face-to-face, but by screaming through canvas), and saw at the entrance of the lot a suntanned and lovely woman, and a man with bright hair and the body of a long-distance runner. The woman looked a little ill. The man wore the white clothes of a peasant, and he carried a sack and two chickens.

Vaggelis went back to his tent and sat in the shade. He took a tin cup from the plastic table with three legs that stood next to his bed. The telegram was still on the stool. Vaggelis looked for something to drink, but Boot walked through garbage and trash and took a bottle from his sack and opened it and poured some ouzo into Vaggelis' cup.

"Vaggelis?" said Boot.

"Would you be pouring me a drink if I weren't?" said Vaggelis.

Vaggelis' eyes had the greenish-yellow tint of olive oil. Boot read the telegram and then crumpled it up and tossed it onto Vaggelis' bed.

"No," said Boot. "We need another stool."

Vaggelis shouted and Theodros brought one. Boot and Mara sat down and Vaggelis stared at Mara's breasts and legs and she glanced at his fat belly and looked through the door of the tent at the hillside beyond the village.

"Christ," said Vaggelis.

Boot had a drink.

"Give me the chickens," said Vaggelis.

"I've come with a guarantee," said Boot.

"Yes," said Vaggelis. "But you should never buy without looking. Give me the chickens."

Boot passed them over. Vaggelis screamed once and Mara stopped studying the hillside. The geek was short and gave the impression of being deformed, although in fact he was not, but he had the thinness of the terminally alcoholic and he trembled. The geek kneeled. His trembling was not exaggerated or spasmodic; it seemed to be evidence of a gentle humming that ran throughout his body. He was dirty, or more than dirty, as though the crusted circles on his face and arms were produced rather than acquired. His hair and beard were thin and greasy, and there were bugs crawling on his scalp and along the seborrheic patches on his face. One ear was cauliflowered, and his nose looked as if it had been broken more than once and by something more than just flesh and bone: iron or a piece of pipe. His eyes were soft and mild and reassuring; it was as though he gazed not from a state of mind (such as peacefulness or serenity), but from stone or sunlight, gold or ice.

It's because he's alive and no longer exists, because there's simply nothing left.

"Here, geek," said Vaggelis.

The geek put the chicken's head into his mouth, bit it off, and (while staring at Boot with that same mild and engaging quality) began to chew. The bird jerked and the wings flapped, but the geek held it in his quaking hands, let the blood run over his fingers and along the undersides of his forearms. It collected in the elbows of his shirt, fell onto his pants (stitched rags, patched and stained). The geek stopped chewing and opened his mouth, and (either because of a trick he had learned or because of the confused agony of nerves) the chicken's beak opened once as though squawking. The geek closed his mouth and Boot and Mara could hear the sound of the beak breaking: a light and delicate snap, like someone stepping on a peanut shell. The bird trembled and flapped its wings and was still. The corners of the geek's eyes were filled with a yellow crust, the eyelids lined with a white slime, bits of which drifted across one cornea. Vaggelis drank. The geek chewed and swallowed: eyes, brains, feathers.

"Here, geek," said Vaggelis.

The geek took the second bird, but this time he turned that same engaging and maddening expression on Mara. He added both feet and put the bird on the ground next to the other. His jaws worked. A bug crawled on his forehead. Mara returned the gaze with an unhidden sexuality, an open invitation, a smiling readiness that would have won over and seduced and captured almost any man. The geek swallowed.

"Here, geek," said Vaggelis. He reached farther into his tent and took a bottle from beneath his cot. "Here."

The geek's fingers left bloodstains on the clear glass. Bubbles rose in the ouzo as the geek drank. He took the bottle and moved away on his knees. Vaggelis belched. The geek sat on a pile of garbage and drank while two dogs looked for something to eat. The children were gone. Boot and Mara looked at the birds, the stains, and Vaggelis. The geek moved between the tents, around the lot, and with an unexpected suddenness appeared for a moment at Boot's side. The gaze was still distant and serene, appealing and outrageous. The geek moved away again, and Vaggelis looked at Boot and said, "So you're the one who's caused all the trouble."

"I haven't caused any trouble," said Boot. "It was already there."

Vaggelis chuckled and said, "For a fact."

"Here," said Boot. He held out fifteen hundred.

Vaggelis ignored the money and said, "How's my friend?"

"I didn't think he had any friends," said Boot, glancing once at the gray paper on Vaggelis' unmade cot.

"Maybe not," said Vaggelis.

"Take the money," said Boot. "My arm's getting tired."

The bills were gone. Vaggelis never took money: it seemed as though he absorbed it. Boot was amazed that a man of Vaggelis' size could move so quickly, so amazed in fact that he still held out his hand, because even though he knew the bills were gone, he had never felt them being removed.

Vaggelis gestured toward Mara.

"I want to fuck your girlfriend," said Vaggelis.

"What?" said Mara.

"Nothing," said Boot. "The arrangement was for fifteen hundred. You have it."

Vaggelis nodded and said, "I know, too, that it's important for the carnival to arrive."

Boot looked at Mara, watched her move uneasily in her clothes.

"They're very angry," said Vaggelis.

"So am I," said Boot.

"That's why it's so important," said Vaggelis. "I want to fuck her."

Boot sat on the stool and smelled the stench of Vaggelis and looked at the birds. *Now I know why Thymos' Renault moved so quickly, why Costas and Pavlos looked so stricken at the advice of the opium smuggler, why no one would ever try to strike a bargain with him. Ever.*

The geek sat next to Mara's stool. The sunlight struck her face, threw into relief the deep angel's kiss above the center of her lips. Boot began to laugh, and Vaggelis looked at Mara in a plainly lascivious way.

"No," said Boot. "You received a telegram."

Vaggelis grunted.

"Let's talk about opium," said Boot.

"Go away, geek," said Vaggelis.

"Why should he send a telegram?" said Boot.

Vaggelis shrugged.

"He's an old friend," said Vaggelis.

"He doesn't have any friends," said Boot. "He's in business. And since you travel, and since he sent you a telegram, you're in business, too."

"Did he tell you?" said Vaggelis.

"Be serious," said Boot. "Were you born in France?"

Vaggelis kicked at one of the chickens.

"That knowledge alone should be guarantee enough to send you to China in a hand basket," said Boot.

Vaggelis looked like a plastic inflatable version of himself, a rubber man into which someone had blown too much air: his eyes bulged and watered.

"But there's more," said Boot.

Vaggelis kicked at the birds.

"I was curious about that," said Vaggelis.

"I'll bet," said Boot. "Give me fifteen hundred."

Boot drank and passed the bottle to Mara.

"I don't want to fuck your girlfriend," said Vaggelis. "I have old habits."

"Give me the fifteen hundred," said Boot.

"Between us," said Vaggelis, "it's bad business to travel without a guarantee."

"You have one," said Boot. "I don't talk much."

The money reappeared, was pushed into Boot's hand with the speed and adroitness of an old-time pickpocket who doesn't have to worry about getting caught.

"Well?" said Vaggelis.

"Ask the opium smuggler when you get there," said Boot. "There's a boat that leaves at ten tonight."

"That's all?" said Vaggelis.

"All," said Boot. "You're lucky I didn't charge you another five hundred for not telling the opium smuggler you're a fool."

Vaggelis held out his cup, and Boot took the bottle from Mara and filled it.

"Do you speak English?" said Boot.

"A little," said Vaggelis.

"If you wanted to fuck her," said Boot, "you should have asked her yourself."

Boot drank and looked at Vaggelis and said to Mara, "Let's go."

They walked away from the tent and through the garbage. Boot stopped and turned and said to Vaggelis, "At ten."

Vaggelis sat in his tent and shouted, told the carnival to break camp, threw the dead birds into the lot. He called the palm reader a slut and told her to get tickets for the ten o'clock boat. Hungry dogs began to eat the birds.

"Some carnival," said Mara.

"What did you expect?" said Boot. "Barnum and Bailey?"

Boot held the sack with the last bottle. They walked past white buildings. Boot fingered the fifteen hundred.

Never, never. Goddamn. He used me better than I could have used myself, because he had me humiliate his partner or cohort or whatever Vaggelis is into his own profit. Five of us will know about the opium, and it always helps to have one less.

Boot watched the slight quiver in Mara's cheeks, the gentle movement of her breasts as she walked over cobblestones. At the waterfront they sat in a taverna beneath a tree and drank. Splashes of light revealed the girlish down on Mara's thighs.

"You have the fifteen hundred back," said Mara.

Boot looked at the reddish bank notes.

"Then we can take a room," said Mara.

"Yes," said Boot. "I brought money for that anyway."

The geek kneeled next to their table. There were feathers and blood around his lips, stuck in his frail beard. Mara allowed the steady gaze, since it was like being examined by a wall. Boot took the last bottle from the sack and gave it to the geek. Mara was fixed in her chair. The geek took the bottle and drank and walked out of the taverna and sat on the curb. He dozed and drank in the sunlight.

"It's a good geek," said Boot.

The clerk at the island's only hotel had a face that looked as though it were part of a bust made by a bad and hurried sculptor: it was lumpish and sagging, and it had the color of reddish clay. His coat was dirty but well pressed. The last entry in the register was two months old. The clerk was dazed and a little confused: his wife had been seduced by the high-wire man. He had seen the palm reader. And now he sat as though counting heartbeats: he lingered over the odor that had come from between the palm reader's legs. The empty hotel didn't make any sense.

The geek sat on the steps just beyond the door.

"Do you have a room?" said Boot.

"Is hell hot?" said the clerk.

"How much?" said Boot.

"Be serious," said the clerk. "I don't want any money."

He slid a key across the counter, walked through the door, and spoke gently to the geek. Boot was left standing with the brightly colored bills in his hand.

The room was on the second floor, and it was large and airy and had a bed, a chair, a bureau, and a bathroom: it was the best room in the hotel. It was a little dusty, but it had a view of the harbor and doors that opened onto a small terrace. The walls were covered with paper, small printed flowers, curled leaves. The doors of the terrace were open and white curtains were filled like sails by the harbor breeze. Boot's clothes were on the chair. Mara undressed slowly. Boot smelled the dust in the room, the slight odor from beneath Mara's arms. Air moved across her breasts, tightened nipples. The bed was an old one and it creaked: the sound was both shabby and rich, evidence of transient loneliness, joy, and misery, of the lopsided sleep of traveling salesmen, the curled embrace of newlyweds, the blind-backed rest of the indifferent. Mara's hand touched the corded surface of the counterpane. Boot saw a scratch on the bureau, a crack in the window of the door that opened onto the terrace. Mara's thigh moved against the side of Boot's face. The skin seemed so smooth as to be covered with a fine powder. She tasted of dry flowers. Boot saw, for a moment, a thin strand of vaginal fluid; it was warm and as clear and slick as egg white. His penis was veined and swollen. Mara took the ridged tip, spread her hair on his stomach, caressed him with it: the hair felt like a piece of cool silk. Boot saw the printed flowers, leaves, a crack in the ceiling, the dusty mirror above the bureau. The bed creaked. The hotel was empty. The floor was covered with a worn carpet; there was a path from the door to the bed and from there to the bathroom. Boot licked the skin behind her knees, felt a vein laboring there. He pulled her hips next to his chest, ran his tongue along her thigh. Mara looked at the cracked glass, the harbor beyond it, the cool water. Boot sucked at the hair at the nape of her neck. He smelled the dust in the room, felt her moisture on his lips, remembered the sharpness in dry flowers, her urine. Mara's breasts were covered by her own and Boot's perspiration, seemed immersed in undulant light. Boot squeezed the brass bars of the bed, saw in tarnished reflection his face, Mara's streaked hair. She put her tongue in the center of his neck. Boot saw the cracked glass, the mirror, the worn spots on the flowered rug, Mara's face, her closed eyes, a tic in her cheek. White curtains billowed. A door slapped against the wall. The cracked glass rattled.

She was asleep. Boot looked at the clock in the square, tried to see the minute hand move. There was a crease in the water, a gold channel that led to the horizon, the burnished disk on it: it looked as though the sea had nurtured and given birth to the sun. Boot watched Mara, now sprawled on the bed, one leg drawn up. He took her clothes and smoothed them as well as he could with his hands, hung the blouse on the back of the chair, put her shoes together in front of it, neatly folded her underwear.

*   *   *

From a distance it sounded like a man walking with a pocketful of change in a pair of baggy pants, and when Boot went to the terrace he saw what seemed to be a segmented and bulky creature making its way down the darkened waterfront: the carnival was contained in three carts drawn by jackasses. Everything squeaked and rattled, the harnesses and bits, pots and pans, the overburdened springs that had been taken from American cars. The sides of the procession were defined by lanterns that hung from each wagon: the carnival emerged from the distance in swaying and golden light. No space was wasted. The fact that clothes and ikons, cots and blankets, chairs and tables, the equipment needed for each act, could be loaded into such a meager amount of space seemed to be some sleight of hand, a trick that required more skill than picking pockets or pulling birds from a hat. The last jackass was tethered to the next wagon and the next animal to the next wagon and the first jackass was led by the man who couldn't speak. The animals' eyes were golden membranes. The palm reader sat next to her immaculate tent. Boot could see the bright thread. The acrobat, the magician, and the high-wire man were drunk and they sang and shouted obscenities at any islander who had the misfortune to be strolling along the waterfront. The geek sat in the cart that carried his pen. He appeared to be nothing more than another bump on the beast that moved toward the ship. The acrobat's dog sat with the acrobat, and it growled and snapped. Vaggelis walked and thanked the men on the waterfront for their patronage. The acrobat, the magician, and the high-wire man demanded that their bastards be given a proper education, boasted of the number of women they had seduced, explained that they had coaxed the women into sleeping with the acrobat's dog as well, pointed out that the animal had fucked more women than any man on the island. Those who watched the departing carnival accepted the abuse with an almost Catholic sense of atonement, as though the carnival weren't simply flesh and blood, but the acidic phantoms of purgatory. Most of those who watched were men who had seen the palm reader, had slept with her and asked for advice about livestock (". . . the little goat with the running sore"), women (". . . she hasn't spoken for a year"), relatives, futures for children yet to be conceived or born (let alone surviving): they were the most spirited of islanders.

Boot went into the street. The carnival had almost reached the ship. The shouting and the banging of pots and pans seemed hallucinatory. Boot walked in the opposite direction.

"Are you with the carnival?" said the girl.

The harbor was a watery cul-de-sac. Boot walked to the end of town and found a chair in a deserted taverna. The sky was glassine, slick: the moon rose, became ringed, looked as white as plaster. Boot's shadow gathered around his feet like some black, casually shed garment. Sound moved across the harbor: winches squealed, Vaggelis shouted, the carts swung from booms. Boot tilted the bottle, watched the moonlight in ouzo.

"Yes," said Boot.

Boot sat at the edge of the taverna, near the opening of a small side street. The cloth looked more black than blue: Boot saw the hem of a school uniform at the corner of a whitewashed building.

"In a way," said Boot.

The fruit vendor stepped out of the side street.

"I was watching them leave," said the girl.

"At ten," said Boot.

Her hand gently touched the whitewashed wall.

"I wanted to," said the girl.

"But you didn't," said Boot.

"No," said the girl. "But you're leaving tonight and you're with them." The girl stepped back into the alley. "I don't want to be seen," she said.

Boot followed her around the corner and up the alley. She stopped at the door of a warehouse that at one time had sheltered stores shipped from ports as far away as India, that had once been fragrant, redolent of cloth on the bolt, of tea and rope and new metal, the hard aura of bounty that surrounds any collection of the recently made or harvested, but was now empty and imposing. It had last been used as a storehouse for charcoal, and its very emptiness made more distinct Boot's sense of himself and the girl. Just walking through it, in it, produced a specific excitement. The girl closed the door: they had to touch each other in the darkness. The girl walked to a window, took off her dress, and hung it on a nail. The walls were black with charcoal. Boot took off his clothes. The girl touched the wall with her fingers, watched, pointed to the floor where there was a pile of clean cotton sacks. She had slight hips, a slender waist, adolescent breasts, thick and heavy hair: in the light from the window she looked like marble on black velvet, the charcoal-covered wall.

"Here," said the girl.

"What about a child?" said Boot.

"There's an old woman," said the girl, "a sorceress."

"But she might want money," said Boot.

"I don't want any money," said the girl.

The window had two crossed sashes: the light lay on the floor in rhomboidal patterns. The sacks had been washed and they smelled of soap and clear air, but even though .

clean, they still had a grayish tint, the uneradicable stain of charcoal. The girl's buttocks and shoulder blades were marked: she had leaned against the wall. They sat on the rags, motionless and pale, cast by light into ivory figures. Boot felt the space, saw the black walls. The girl was tentative but curious: she looked at him for a moment, reached between his legs, and Boot felt her fingers as they probed, examined, caressed. Boot kissed the back of her shoulder, then realized that there was charcoal on his lips. He left a mark wherever he touched her. The girl examined his chest and arms, pulled at the flesh along his side, moved her fingers over his thighs and calves. Boot bit at the hair beneath her arms. Her breasts and stomach were covered with the faint shadow of Boot's lips, the dusty charcoal. She was surprised and awkward: Boot touched her between her legs and she jumped, opened her thighs. His hands were sooty, too, and fingerprints showed like dark bruises on her arms, along her side, on her cheeks. *How am I going to get that off.* She was wet and she gazed at Boot with frank curiosity and said, "So that's what it is."

In the silent space Boot heard a sound like someone using a dishrag, her slight breathing, the rustling of the sacks. One breast, her neck, half of her face, were bright and milky: her lips and the one visible nipple were black. She was as gentle and caressing as the island air, perhaps because she had grown up in it, because it had filled her first breath. She touched him behind the neck, drew him against her, held him and was more gentle and natural than any woman he had known. It made him aware of his own coarseness, his acquired brutality.

She touched the tip of a finger to her tongue and rubbed a spot of soot from his face.

"I remember you," said the girl.

"From a year ago," said Boot.

"Yes," said the girl. "From before. Here."

She stood and walked to her dress. Boot watched her fluid gait, heard the diminutive sound of her bare feet on the concrete floor.

"Here," she said. "The coin you threw me. A year ago."

Boot sat in shocked immobility, more aware than ever of the silent space.

"Here," she said.

The silver coin glowed in the moonlight, looked as though it had been cast not by men, by stone molds and hard stampings, but by neutral elements, bland air and water.

"Take it," said the girl.

What can she spend it on.

He took the coin and went to his pants and dropped it into a pocket.

The girl looked at Boot and said, "Don't be a fool. It was just anyone."

"It's not that," said Boot.

"You look frightened," said the girl.

Boot laughed and said, "Yes. How am I going to get you clean?"

"I brought a cloth," said the girl.

She took it from the pocket of her dress and gave it to Boot.

"Stand on the sacks and don't touch anything," said Boot.

Boot touched the cloth with his tongue and then scrubbed gently at the spots on her face. The girl had never stood before a man, but she did so now without modesty or vanity: she simply allowed herself to be cleaned. Boot touched her breasts and arms, wet the cloth again, tried to conserve each small bit of fabric. A thin stream of fluid ran from her genitals: in the light it looked like crude oil on white and polished stone.

Boot licked the cloth again, tasted the soot, looked at the girl's skin and saw that it was now more gray than white.

"This will never do," said Boot. "Look."

He touched her breast and neck, pointed at the inside of her thigh.

"We're at the end of town now," said Boot. "Is there someplace . . ."

"Yes," said the girl. "Will you watch?"

The girl put on her dress, the dark cloth seemed severe and confining, an institutional shroud. Boot felt the coin in his pocket. The girl unlatched the door and they walked into the alley. A path, smooth and packed earth, led from the end of the quay. The girl moved quickly, glancing once over her shoulder, not so much to see if Boot was following but for fear of exposure. Insects squeaked and hummed in the grass. They climbed down rocks onto a recessed and pebbly beach. Boot held the girl's dress, and she swam in the dark water marked by the phosphorescence of her wake. Her splashing was no louder than the half-foot waves that broke on the beach. She stood before Boot, cupping water over her breasts and stomach, running wet hands over her thighs, scrubbing her ankles and knees with sand. Light that seemed as unctuous and clear as baby oil spread over her moving back.

"Did anyone see?" said the girl.

The air was warm, the girl waited for her skin to dry. They stood beneath the bluff. The girl took her dress, and Boot followed her working hips as they climbed the path away from the beach. The lights of the ship, the clock in the square, and the darkened hotel were visible from the top of the ridge. Boot stood with the girl in the alley and touched her wet and shiny hair.

"It'll be all right," said the girl.

Mara came around the corner and saw them and walked directly to Boot and slapped him once and then again and spat in his face. The girl instinctively left. Boot heard the sound of her feet on the cobblestones. He wiped the spittle from his face, tasted it on his lips.

The geek had left the ship and was now sitting on the steps of the hotel. Boot and Mara climbed the stairs to their room.

"You're sooty," said Mara.

Boot took off his clothes and stood in front of her. Mara took his penis into her mouth, sucked, caressed his testicles, stopped and looked at him, and said, "I can taste the soot. And the girl. A little blood."

Mara took off her underwear and pulled up her skirt and sat at the edge of the bed. She didn't want to stain her skirt. Boot was immediately aware of the difference between the girl and Mara, sharp bones, the oval and pubescent dip and opening and the stronger and lush hips and legs of a woman, the girl's tentative and gentle movements, Mara's drawn rocking. The geek moaned on the steps, the bed creaked. Boot could smell the girl on his fingers. Mara's hands lay on the white counterpane: the fingers were extended, arched, and the lines of the palm were red and stark. She looked at Boot and shook her head and slapped him.

"You didn't have to do that," said Boot.

There was a little soot on Mara's lip.

"You'd be surprised," said Mara.

Boot sat on the chair before her.

"Did I stop you?" said Mara.

176

"I'm going to take a shower," said Boot.

"Did I?" said Mara.

"From coming?" said Boot. "Yes."

"Good," said Mara.

Boot stood under the warm and soft water. *We've got to make the boat, it's almost ten.* He stood under the water only for a moment and then took a towel.

Mara sat in the doorway on a chair and said, "What was the girl like?"

"Maybe I should have brought her up here," said Boot, "and we both could have had her. You like a little now and then, don't you?"

Mara went into the bathroom.

"They're going to kill you," she said.

"No," said Boot. "They're more clever than that. We're going to miss the boat."

Boot left the key on the counter of the hotel, and he and Mara walked along the waterfront. The geek followed them, sometimes crawling on his knees in the gutter, always a few paces behind, always watching with an open and infuriating gaze. Boot still carried the sack.

"Do you want an orange?" said Boot.

"No," said Mara.

Boot dropped the sack into a trash can.

There were splashy circles of light on the ship's deck where the carnival had settled. Lanterns hissed. The wagons had been tied fast and the jackasses had been led on board. The acrobat's dog was tied to a wagon tongue. Vaggelis leaned against the railing, still bidding farewell to those who had come as far as the ship's moorings. The geek followed Mara and Boot up the gangplank and between the wagons into the center of the carnival. The wagons were arranged as

177

though Vaggelis were expecting an attack by Indians. The acrobat, the palm reader, and the strongman sat with blankets over their shoulders. The magician had a stool. Theodros had bread and cheese, and he began cutting it into eight equal parts, even though no one looked hungry.

"It's a good carnival," said Vaggelis to Boot.

"I can see that," said Boot.

The geek stood next to Boot and Mara.

"Next year! Next year!" screamed Vaggelis. He waved to the last of the islanders as the ship cleared its moorings and headed for sea: black sky and water, both rich with stars. Mara went to their room and Boot walked to the stern of the ship, where he could see the skeletal wake, calcimine and brilliant, as though it were composed of the finely granulated bones of fish, bones now mixed with points of starlight which gave the ship the aspect of gliding not through water and air but galactic space, both dark and pierced, the ship seeming earthbound only in the banging of tin and the humming of guy wires, the voices and rustling of passengers, the wash of water against the bow, the odor of salty mist. The geek pulled on Boot's sleeve and offered a bottle. Boot took it and then the geek was gone. The wake could have been drawn with a ruler: it led directly to the lights of Ikaria.

Vaggelis came around the corner from the bridge and walked to the railing at the stern.

"So," said Vaggelis, "now we can talk."

"Thanks for the bottle," said Boot.

"It didn't come from me," said Vaggelis, "but from the punk who runs the chicken lottery."

"Thank him," said Boot.

"I don't talk to scum like that," said Vaggelis.

Boot watched as the lights of the island disappeared: it

looked as though the celestial sphere had turned, as though an even and flat and varicolored line of stars had dropped below the horizon.

"No one can hear," said Vaggelis. "Let's have it."

"We can't talk," said Boot.

Boot could smell Vaggelis even in the sea air.

"That's the point," said Boot. "The fact that I won't talk, not even to you who will be protected by my not saying what you should and will know. Because if I won't even speak to you, then you can rest assured that I'll speak to no one."

Vaggelis shook his head and laughed, slapped Boot on the back, and said, "Don't be funny."

"No," said Boot, "maybe you won't be told anything. Maybe you'll be asked to go on as before. It always helps to have one less."

"Isn't that the truth," said Vaggelis.

"Too bad you're not a murderer," said Boot.

Vaggelis laughed, messed up Boot's hair, and said, "Yes, to be sure. It's a shame," and then walked back toward the bridge.

Boot stood at the rail. Vaggelis' stench lingered. Boot poked a finger at a life ring, felt his fingers penetrate the frangible interior, the rotting and buoyant substance there. The acrobat and the strongman walked along the rail, passed the bridge, their legs showed in the turning circle of light from the gimbal lantern. The wake made a sound like a waterfall. Boot held the bottle by its neck. The acrobat and the strongman moved from the bridge to the stern, breathing deeply and stretching, apparently trying to sober up, but they separated and approached, one on the starboard rail, one on the port. Boot could see through the glassed-in bridge a ship's officer drinking coffee, obviously fixed on the approaching sea, looking for lighted buoys, fishermen's boats, the tip of some neglected peak. The strongman stood next to a lifeboat covered with a tarp that was as tight as a drumhead. Boot could feel the engines working below deck, the vibration of the screw. A jackass brayed on the forward deck. Boot saw the acrobat's hand on the rail, the strongman's heavy movements.

It's one thing to gamble, and it's another to be a fool.

The strongman stepped into the center of a neatly coiled line and said, "Shit," and the acrobat moved quickly, but Boot was already standing in the light from the bridge.

"Good night," said Boot. "Enjoy the air."

The strongman said, "Shit."

Boot stepped into the hatch and went down the corridor. Mara was sitting on the bed.

"Hello," said Boot.

He locked the door.

"What's that for?" said Mara.

"Just leave it that way," said Boot.

"I'm not going anyplace," said Mara.

Boot sat next to Mara, took off his clothes, and said, "I'm tired."

Mara touched his hair, put her light lips against his shoulder. They heard the plunging of the pistons in the engine room, the beginnings of an argument on the forward deck, the dark wash of the Aegean. Mara took off her clothes and lay next to Boot, curled her legs against his bent knees, pressed her buttocks and back against his thighs, stomach, and chest, allowed him to caress her hair, to touch the nape of her neck with his lips.

Boot laughed.

"What?" said Mara.

"It's only the little things that would be worth knowing," said Boot, "if there were some way of doing it."

Stock prices would be handy, or the results of horse races or maybe the weather and perhaps the final standings of each season's soccer and football teams. The knowledge of anything more personal about the future would make the entire spectacle seem one dull sentence served on death row.

Boot felt the movement of Mara's ribs, a gentle beating in her chest. Because even though Boot had dealt and bargained with what he thought were reasonable expectations, it was thinking, metabolism realized, that provided a buzzing sense of wonder, of men and women and things known and controlled, at least partially, which is to say known and not stripped of all mystery.

One or two surprises and that'll do it. Everyone's getting a little skittish after the opium smuggler's advice. So a few more bits and they'll send us off with a brass band. All I need is time, a little luck, and a clear head.

Boot woke once as the ship rolled in swollen seas, felt Mara swaying against him, heard the timbers protest (as much against the distance of land, the alien sea, as the pressure on the hull), then slept again, finding only the reeled and slick-minded rest of an alcoholic. The ship was jarred by the quay on Samos and Boot saw Mara now dressed and looking through the porthole. She pulled at Boot's ankle and said, "It's already started."

It was almost dawn: the sky was still cavernous, the light still blue. The preparations were meager, so much so, in fact, that anyone unfamiliar with the island would have missed them altogether. There were a few extra lights, some of which were colored, strands of crepe paper hanging from the verandas of the houses that faced the waterfront, paper that looked as though it had been used before, and it gave the quay an aura of excitement already spent rather than of anticipation a year in the making. But the atmosphere had changed; even though it was four thirty of the day before the night of the carnival, there were fishermen who were already drunk and singing, and no one seemed to mind. The quay appeared blessed because so many people were thinking about it, whether turning slowly in their beds or already laboring in the fields.

Boot dressed and walked with Mara onto the deck. The man who ran the chicken lottery passed Boot and said, "A good geek." The geek stood next to Boot, grasped the railing, and gazed at the islanders who had waited up to catch the first glimpse of the carnival.

"A good geek," said the man. He smiled at Boot and walked below deck, toward the gangplank.

Vaggelis said to Boot, "Chicken lotteries, punk."

Boot and Mara walked through the carnival. The high-wire man said to the acrobat, "Too bad the cunt isn't as good-looking."

The deck hands were quick about their business. Already the wagons were free of lines and the cranes were beginning to work. The livestock had been led to the quay. The members of the carnival filed silently down the gangplank, and only the magician acknowledged, with a slight smile, the appreciative silence of the fifty or so people who had assembled at the side of the ship. The geek followed Boot down to the quay.

Costas' face seemed to be hung on hooks: a day and a night of worry hadn't done much good.

"So," said Costas, pulling at Boot's sleeve, "we're going to have a carnival after all."

Boot looked at the jaundiced fingers, the nicotine stains that were as yellow as old newspaper.

"Yes," said Boot.

Boot fumbled in his pocket and revealed for an instant the fifteen hundred.

"I see you have the lights up," said Boot.

"Wait," said Costas.

"And decorations," said Boot.

It looked as though Costas were having a heart attack: the sudden perspiration on his forehead reflected the bluish light.

"Ask," said Boot, "if you're so curious."

"Vaggelis never goes anywhere without a guarantee," said Costas.

"He got a guarantee," said Boot.

Vaggelis moved away from the side of the ship, through the goats and wagons, the jackasses and chickens.

"What's that, then?" said Costas, pointing to Boot's shirt pocket.

Boot shrugged.

"What's this about a guarantee?" said Vaggelis.

"He doesn't think you got one," said Boot.

"I got one," said Vaggelis to Costas. "Why the fuck else do you think I'd be here?"

But Costas was unconvinced, even though he didn't have the backbone or honesty or (what would have been to Costas) foolish gall to say it to Vaggelis' face, nor would he ever have attempted to bring the carnival to Samos without a guarantee: he was unconvinced because for years he had been able to detect the slight change in a man's expression that occurs after having received money, and Costas had become so proficient at it that even Vaggelis, who was above everything else an artist of fraud, couldn't keep the telltale lines from his face.

"I got one," said Vaggelis, who glared once at Boot and walked away and shouted at the deck hands, told them that he'd break more than their miserable necks if so much as a tin cup was dented in moving the wagons from the deck to the quay.

Costas now looked truly frightened, because he had had two warnings, one from the opium smuggler and one from the fact that Vaggelis had arrived on the island without a guarantee. These things were enough to make Costas suspect that if Boot had been able to do something to both the opium smuggler and Vaggelis, then Costas was out of his depth.

"Don't be a fool," said Boot. "He's got a guarantee. That's all you need to know."

Pavlos came out of the crowd, too, and he looked at Costas and then at Boot, and Boot said, "Here. Buy the geek a bottle."

Pavlos took the note without a word, and Costas and Pavlos walked in the direction of Pavlos' taverna, Costas gesticulating and rubbing his head. Pavlos listened, but his head was bent as though he had lost in the gutter some small but valuable possession.

"They've got a bottle for you, geek," said Boot.

The geek walked slowly, moved over the cobblestones with a pinched gait. It seemed as though his abasement were some gentle wind that blew him in any direction pointed out by another. He was beyond concern, living in his body alone, always glancing with that same engaging expression at anyone who happened to pass by. The geek was unaware of the necessity of his existence, if not constantly in one place, on one island, then at least certainly on one island at one time, especially during the carnival, when he crouched in his pen and bit the heads from chickens, ate their feet, or the dung of animals, the scales of fish, the deformed creatures caught in a net, anything at all. He performed for a swallow of liquor. His cup was chained to his pen. There were men who shit in a bag and brought that along as well, but it made no difference. The geek was so far beyond self as to be more than fascinating. The men and women who watched him did so in silence, struck dumb by the spectacle, as though the geek were the animated remains of a saint, something more holy than abasement.

"It's all in the eyes," said Vaggelis. "A blind geek isn't worth a shit."

Because Vaggelis knew that the gaze both infuriated and attracted. It was beyond the understanding of those who watched, because it violated the basis on which the islanders turned both hatred and love on the land and sea: an unbreakable sense of self. It was infuriating that in the midst of abasement there was an elusive peace, something that the farmers and fishermen had felt, but only fleetingly, usually at the end of a season, when surveying a miserable crop, when calculating the number of hungry days in a winter, when they knew they had been beaten but weren't lost, and that they would try again. And so even that fleeting sense of satisfaction, or pride, or realization of ongoing struggle was parodied and outraged, and more outraged than anything else, because some of the farmers weren't sure what was being mocked: it was as though they had come to face a twisted and calm vision from their own worst nightmares of themselves.

Pavlos gave the geek a bottle, and the geek walked to the hotel and leaned against the red car and drank.

185

* * *

Boot stood on the terrace. Mara was fresh from the shower.

"What are you doing?" said Mara.

"Nothing," said Boot.

"Well," said Mara, "if it's nothing, why don't you come inside?"

Boot sat on the bed. Mara stood before him. Boot looked at her stomach, skin that was still wet from the shower, slick and brown, lipped and creased flesh, the interior curve of her buttocks against the sky. Boot took off his clothes. Mara dropped the towel and kneeled before him: her smooth legs lay against the polished floor. She put her wet hair between his legs. The coldness surprised him.

The first clear light filled the room; Boot could see the even definition of Mara's ribs. He nibbled at her breath, held some in his mouth, tasted it.

"What happens to you is your own lookout," said Mara.

She sat with one leg drawn up, her back leaning against the head of the bed, exposing the long and smooth muscles in her legs.

Boot and Mara heard the geek drop his bottle onto the stones of the hotel steps.

"Come on," said Boot. "I want to go home."

Because he should be walking in that direction by now.

"The drive would be nice," said Boot.

"How about a little sleep?" said Mara.

"We haven't got the time," said Boot.

The geek was sleeping on the steps of the hotel. The fishermen were just beginning to bring in the catch. Mara drove through the deserted streets and Boot watched for a pedestrian. The monastery was perched over the sea, appearing to grow out of the rocky projection it rested upon. The building looked like a sculpted stalagmite, a white structure set off by the indistinct mainland and the sea that was as blue as the center of a chemist's flame.

He walks quickly for a fat man, or maybe his curiosity was too much, maybe he started earlier.

Boot began to chuckle.

"What's so funny?" said Mara.

"It's not funny," said Boot.

"Then don't laugh."

Of course: you understand (you? she's right: I've been talking to myself). The clothes are perfect. I'm no different from any fisherman or farmer.

Where is he?

They drove in silence. Boot watched the terraced landscape, the weeds and olive trees, the fields shored up with stones.

"There he is," said Boot. "Stop next to him."

Boot greeted Vaggelis.

"A little early for a walk, isn't it?" said Boot.

"I don't think so," said Vaggelis. "And what was that about a guarantee?"

"I told him you got one."

Vaggelis grunted through his panting; his perspiration was as clear as ouzo. Boot sat on the trunk and put his legs into the jump seat.

"Get in," said Boot. "We'll give you a lift."

Vaggelis looked at the car, the road ahead, and got in.

"You shouldn't have done that," said Vaggelis. "The guarantee."

"I didn't say anything," said Boot. "He saw your face."

Vaggelis shrugged and looked up the road and said, "Christ. That's the worst part about this business. Everyone lives in the middle of nowhere."

Mara parked the car. The opium smuggler sat under a tree. He gazed at the mainland and then at Vaggelis and said, "What took you so long?"

"Try running a carnival," said Vaggelis.

Boot and Mara stood next to Vaggelis.

"We're going to grow it on the island," said the opium smuggler. "He," pointing one deceptively languid finger at Boot, "arranged it."

Showmanship evaporated, and Boot knew why Costas was frightened: Vaggelis looked like a murderer inspecting a rack of recently sharpened knives.

"Will he have a share?" said Vaggelis.

"Yes," said the opium smuggler.

The chickens pecked through the dust in the yard. The eyes of the opium smuggler's dog moved to the lips of each man who spoke, as though words could be eaten.

"I'd say about a fifth," said Boot.

"A fifth," said the opium smuggler.

"A lot," said Vaggelis.

Boot's hands were wet; he picked up some dust.

"It's a fifth of a whole I never saw anyway," said the opium smuggler. "The price I paid on the mainland."

"We've never had . . ." Vaggelis gestured at Boot, opened a hand, grimaced.

"This isn't a convent," said the opium smuggler. "Say what you mean. A foreigner."

"Yes," said Vaggelis.

"Nothing seals lips like money," said the opium smuggler.

Drops of Vaggelis' perspiration fell to the ground, made spots in the island's reddish dust. Mara sat on the exposed root of the tree, pushed the dog's nose away from the space between her legs.

"Shit," said Vaggelis.

"Try getting someone to grow it on the island," said Boot. "It's worth a fifth or more." He looked at the opium smuggler. "But I don't want it."

The opium smuggler gazed across the strait.

"I don't trust men who don't like money," said the opium smuggler.

"No," said Boot, "it's not the money. I'll give my share for something else."

A slight breeze blew through the yard. The dust gathered into small funnels, a strand of hair moved over Mara's face. Boot had never seen the opium smuggler grin before.

"I wonder what that could be," said the opium smuggler.

"A fifth for one more message. One warning," said Boot.

"Yes," said the opium smuggler. "I can understand that. Money wouldn't be much good to a dead man. But then I could just wait and collect anyway."

"Who knows?" said Boot. "Maybe they're scared enough already. Maybe they'll leave me alone. And then I could use the fifth and you'd have nothing I'd want to buy. So it would get messy, and I don't think you like messes. This way you get a clean fifth. They're scared because they don't know what's happening, so I couldn't talk even if I wanted to."

Boot rubbed the dust between his palms, watched as it made a neat conical pile on the ground between his knees. The opium smuggler looked at Mara.

"I'll send it today," said the opium smuggler. "You're out."

"Good," said Boot. "Have him take it."

Boot pointed at Vaggelis.

The opium smuggler nodded.

Boot took Mara by the hand and walked toward the ridge

and his house, but stopped and said, "Wait," and turned. *That's too cheap, he should go himself.* He walked back to the opium smuggler and Vaggelis, who both had their backs to him, who were already arguing, and Boot heard the opium smuggler say, "Don't worry. He'll do it himself."

Boot stopped, turned, and walked back to Mara.

From the top of the ridge they could see the fields, Ulla and her husband working in them, the jackass turning in harness. *At least it's almost harvest, and they'll need some money until the first crop is planted, so they'll have to work awhile longer: it would be too much for them to sit and watch the squash, grapes, and tomatoes rot in the fields.*

Mara sat on the low bed in the study and Boot sat in a chair opposite her and they listened to the hoes working in the earth, the ticking of Boot's wind-up clock.

"I'm taking a nap," said Mara.

She spoke to the wall. Boot felt like a voyeur: she undressed with abrupt carelessness, indifference. Mara twitched in her sleep, the bed creaked. Flies buzzed in the room. A scorpion climbed on the wall. Boot knocked it down and killed it with the bottle.

Mara woke in the early evening.

Boot took off his clothes and lay next to her. He touched her neck with his lips. Her eyes were fixed upon the coast. Boot touched her again and she recoiled as though he had dropped a leech on her breast. Her eyes were still withheld, fixed on a point over Boot's shoulder and beyond the window.

"Well?" said Mara.

Boot shook his head.

"You're lying," said Mara.

She sat with legs akimbo, bound by the sheet. Her face was set with the nonchalant and payday expression usually seen in cheap pornographic photographs. Boot ran his tongue behind her ear.

"Don't touch me," said Mara.

Her eyes returned to the window, the indelible landscape, dissolving now in evening light.

"No," said Boot.

"You're lying," said Mara.

"No," said Boot. "There are things I can do."

"I'm finished," said Mara. "I don't know why I ever let you touch me. You're a drunk. You're disgusting."

Mara pulled on her clothes.

"Did you think you could get off so easily?" said Boot.

"I never struggle," said Mara.

"Of course," said Boot.

Mara stood in the doorway.

"Do something," said Mara.

Boot looked at his empty hands.

"Since you struggle so much," said Mara.

"Did you feel good?" said Boot.

"I can't remember," said Mara.

Mara was gone. Boot listened to her sandals on the terrace, but he didn't watch from the window as she picked her way through the quilted fields. He went into the kitchen and took the first bottle from the shelf and sat on the terrace. From the ridge, beyond the opium smuggler's yard, he heard the engine of a sports car start. The day closed slowly: light was sucked from the east and the island was hooded with blackness, stars.

Boot noticed his anger as much as his hand, the air he breathed, or the fact of sight.

* * *

Boot finished the bottle and climbed the steps to the house of Ulla and her husband. He entered without knocking and found them sitting in front of the unused hearth. There were black, flame-shaped marks on the plaster above it. Ulla and her husband were eating sausage and eggs and bread, and each had a small glass of wine. They looked at Boot once and went back to eating. The door swung on its leather hinges, sounding like a burdened pack saddle. The house was basically one room. There was a bed with a bare mattress and grayish blankets, a waxed and immaculate dresser on which there were doilies and trinkets, small glass bottles, a postcard from America, a photograph from the day of Ulla's wedding. A tin ikon hung on the wall. There were three stools: one for Ulla, one for her husband, and one that served as a table. They ate from metal plates. Pots, pans, a large knife, a spatula, and a cup hung on the wall next to the fireplace. The whitewash had yellowed, and the house was closed by years of lantern vapor. Ulla and her husband had eaten little; most of what lay in the pan on the stool between them was cold and untouched.

"Do you want to eat?" said Ulla.

"No," said Boot.

Ulla took the leftover food and put it in a makeshift larder, a recess in the wall that was covered by a piece of red cloth.

"There's no need," said Boot.

"What?" said the farmer.

"He's lost his slut," said Ulla. She fastened the piece of cloth.

"You don't have to grow it," said Boot.

"You think things can be undone," said Ulla.

"Look at me," said Boot.

192

"You've lost your slut," said Ulla. Her face was cut by shadow: a point of light in a slick eye looked like a star beyond the dark side of a half-moon. The watch now hung from a nail next to the bed.

"Go away," said the farmer, "and keep quiet about what we'll grow."

"It was a cheap watch," said Ulla.

"Yes," said Boot. "What did it cost you?"

Ulla and her husband sat before the hearth. Boot was already stumbling on the steps. He landed at the end of the first short switchback and swore and waited for a moment and then felt the warm moisture in his hair. The light went out in Ulla's house. Boot knew they were already on the mattress, back to back, each staring into half of the house.

Boot went into his kitchen, put two bottles into a sack, opened another, and began to walk through the fields, tripping over the mounds around carefully cultivated vines, navigating by the light he had left burning in his house. He found the jackass and stroked its fur, felt the blinking eyes. The animal was black and still in the light and Boot stood before it as though the jackass were the living altar of everything that is final. The animal flinched when Boot's fingers found the open sores, the marks that had come from the beating, the first day in harness. The fields were covered with the throbbing sound of insects. Boot climbed the ridge, was pleased with himself that he had been able to find his way through the gully without falling once, and walked into the opium smuggler's yard.

Boot kicked at the barking dog.

"You want a drink?" said Boot.

The opium smuggler sat under the tree.

"No," said the opium smuggler.

Boot felt the cold, probing nose of the dog.

"Well?" said Boot.

"You're out," said the opium smuggler. "I sent the message."

Boot sat in the dust.

"The quarantine's lifted," said the opium smuggler. "You could just go home and sleep and leave tomorrow."

The opium smuggler saw the black streak on the side of Boot's face.

"You're bleeding," said the opium smuggler.

"I fell down," said Boot. "No, I think I want to see what that last message did."

"Good," said the opium smuggler. "Go to the carnival."

The opium smuggler was gone, too, and Boot was walking along the road, looking at the terraced fields, the olive trees in moonlight, broken fences that kept nothing in and no one out. The bottle was empty. Boot smashed it, picked up a shattered bit, saw through a biased edge distorted land and sky. The road was filled with white and glowing stones. Every now and then Boot found himself on the ground, searching with numb fingers for his bag.

The courtyard of the monastery was deserted.

"Hello," said Boot.

There was no answer. Boot screamed. The sound hung for a moment in the empty courtyard, then dissolved, bled toward the open terrace, the sea. Boot sat on a chair near the low wall, put his feet on the old stones, leaned back, and drank. The water looked like sluggish oil, dark, quiet, unhurried: there was no wind.

Nicos screamed.

Boot walked through the low archways into the monastery itself, the soles of his shoes echoing on the flat stones. He waited, heard the wail again, and climbed the stairs to the veranda that ran past each of the monks' cells. Boot smelled the salty air, the odor of the olive tree in the center of the terrace, the damp stones he stood on. His hand touched the moss that grew on a permanently shaded wall. The silence of the monastery was as oppressive as the vows of the monks who lived there.

Scream, scream. I can't tell where you are if you don't scream.

Boot saw a spreading patch of light from a door at the end of the veranda. He walked in a narrow corridor of nausea, holding one bottle and clutching the bag that held the other. He drank whenever he felt the sickness, the eruption of cold and heat that came so quickly they seemed to be one and the same. Water bugs, each half a foot long, moved on the stones. Boot labored in the humiliation of alcohol, liquor that now produced the sense of entrapment it had originally been taken to relieve. Boot could hear the scaled bodies of the insects being dragged along the veranda, the squeak of lubricated joints.

Nicos screamed, and Boot stood outside the door, swaying gently, suddenly being concerned about his appearance, but then remembered Nicos was incapable of seeing just people and objects, shorn of sunbursts, tentacles, lizards climbing from pockets, rats eating cheeks.

The hinges had been made by hand, and the door opened with the sound of wrenched metal. The distillate of violence hung in the cell: it was as though Boot had pried open the door of a wrecked automobile. Nicos shrieked, jumped from his cot, and squatted in a corner. His old limbs trembled and sagged, revealed the fleshy magnetism of the grave. Boot stood before him. Nicos shrieked, kneeled, made a cross with his arms, begged.

Boot sat on the cot and moved only to take a drink from the bottle. Nicos rocked back and forth, cradled himself with his arms. There was a pack of cards on the nightstand, a rough and unfinished table that had been made by the monk, a table that would have been unsteady anywhere else in the world but stood firmly because of the uneven floor of the cell. Nicos had been able to make it fit because of the hours he had spent on his hands and knees examining each stone and crack. Boot put down the sack and bottle and picked up the deck.

"Cards," said Boot.

Boot held up the deck and took the fifteen hundred from his pocket. Nicos' eyes were still covered by a glaze that any potter would give a leg for, but he stopped shrieking. Froth and saliva oozed from one side of his mouth. He looked at the bright bank notes and the cards.

"You're drooling," said Boot.

Boot took a damp cloth from the floor and wiped the old monk's lips.

"There," said Boot. "I think you feel better now."

Nicos made the entire cell resonant with a cry.

"Easy," said Boot. "How are we going to play cards if you keep on like that?"

A hand struggled through palsy for a gambler's gesture, the neat alignment of fingers. The veins were almost verdant, as though they were filled with pond scum.

"What's it going to be?" said Boot.

Nicos struck and grabbed at the cards, knocked them over the stones, and then jumped away from the bright ones, kings, queens, and jacks: they seemed animate and threatening, a deck of scorpions rather than cards. Nicos' hands rested on his bald and wrinkled scalp.

"What are you doing?" said Lukas.

The door struck the dark wall of the veranda. Boot was gathering the cards. Lukas pulled him from the cell.

"Wait," said Boot.

"Get out of here," said Lukas.

Boot held the fifteen hundred in his hand.

"Get out."

Boot looked at his sack and bottle. They still sat next to Nicos' cot.

"No," said Boot. "I want my sack."

"He's an old man," said Lukas.

Boot could see the furious eyes in the habit.

"Give me my sack," said Boot.

"I warned you," said Lukas.

"My sack," said Boot.

"Oh," said Lukas, "you mean your liquor. Here."

Nicos sat in the corner, drooling again, becoming frightened of his own saliva as it dripped across his arm, agonized that it touched him, but too frightened to wipe it off, too disoriented even to know that it could be wiped off.

"Why don't you go to the carnival?" said Lukas.

He closed the door and pushed Boot down the veranda. Boot became confused in the darkness, dropped the fifteen hundred, stumbled against the stone parapet. Boot held the bottle and bag and searched.

"Here it is," said Lukas.

He stuck the money into Boot's pocket.

Boot found the stairs and then the courtyard. The night was touched with glowing bits: Boot shook his head, drank against the sickness, knew that he was shaking by the sound of the brown paper sack.

The church was illuminated by candles burning in an ornate holder, a tripod with elaborate figures on its legs. The tripod held a bowl that was filled with dirt. The dirt supported the candles. Boot took one and walked from ikon to ikon, examining the detailed saints, bearded and haloed, dressed in long gowns, caught in tooled gold. The glass that covered the ikons was marked by lips, in candlelight the residue seemed whitish and soft, as though the images of lips had been drawn with the dust of moths' wings. Boot put down his sack and bottle and kissed the ikons, the smudges made by previous mouths, touching and reaching not for ikons so much as for the places where others had humbled themselves, those spots where islanders had paid homage to mysteries that oppressed them. The candle was the color of jaundiced flesh: the congealed wax on Boot's hand looked like stilled larvae. Boot kissed the glass, the smudges, believed them to be evidence of the pure monstrosity of the island, believed, too, that it was the marks that made the images holy. Most of the smudges were over the gold. Boot turned quickly and saw something recede into the cracks of the neatly fitted stones of the floor. It was as though the ikons themselves were burning: in the light of the candle the faces dripped and ran, scowled and collapsed. A rat left the sanctuary of a monk's chair and crawled into the corner of the church. Boot saw the drops of its urine. His lips made a slight smacking sound that filled the empty space, the high-domed ceiling. The sound echoed on walls built from the columns of ancient temples.

"Get out of here," said Lukas.

Boot searched for the bottle and bag.

"I was just leaving," said Boot.

He was on the road again, picking his way through weathered gullies and over stones, still walking in a path narrowly delineated by nausea. Boot sat for a moment and then jumped, twisted back into the road, because the grass was filled with bugs, large and grotesque creatures, winged and scaled; each head was as large as an almond. Boot hit one with the bottle and it screamed, squeaked, made a noise like some piece of electrical equipment gone amok. The entire field revealed itself: each stalk was occupied, and Boot could hear glassine wings being rubbed together, jaws devouring vegetation and other creatures, the drip of juices from severed limbs. He could feel them climbing in his clothes and he stood in the middle of the road and slapped at his sleeves and pant legs, no longer concerned about leaving on his skin the smashed guts of any creature. Movement drew them. The insects' scales were a milky green and they had the luminescence of mother-of-pearl. The wings, legs, and triangular heads made a necklace of sensation: Boot felt them at the top of his chest, beneath his ears and chin. He cleaned himself with the bag and took the bottle and was farther up the road, running, not even bothering to look over his shoulder.

He began to walk again, but he could still hear the insects. The second bottle was empty, and Boot threw it in the direction of the noise, which is to say it didn't matter where he threw it, since the noise seemed to be coming from himself.

"It'll go away," said Boot. "I just have to wait."

In the gullies there were moving rocks, toads and lizards. Boot stepped on one and said, "Shit. I should have brought a lantern."

The toads were large and they had the same coloring as the dirt and stones. Their evolution was perfect: they could be seen only when they moved. Boot heard the muscles and tendons sliding beneath horned skin, watched as the stones moved up the road or slid toward the fields. Boot picked up a stone: it seemed light and dry, but he couldn't find its eyes so he threw it into a field.

The paved section of the road undulated slowly. It was warm and at first Boot thought it was the heat from the sun, but then he touched it and was convinced that blood ran beneath the asphalt. The road oozed and gave at each step, and Boot squatted and vomited, held his legs against his chest, became too terrified to move. *It'll go away if I just wait. If I just wait I won't have to look at it anymore.* His hands were wet and he rubbed the moisture between thumb and forefinger, but the moisture seemed to form a thin and shiny membrane. He could feel it leaking from beneath his arms, covering his skin. The scrub brush moved. Boot shook his head and screamed through vomit, then closed his eyes and saw things worse than bugs or sliding toads and stones. He wiped his hands on the bag, used it to clean his shirt and mouth, stood and began to walk.

He could see the stars clearly.

"Fine," said Boot.

He drank from the last bottle and walked downhill. Lights were strung around the edge of the waterfront; the quarter-moon of bulbs was cheerful and hideous. The harbor was decorated, too. The fishermen had hung colored lanterns from the masts of their boats, and the flat expanse of water looked like the spot where a liquid rainbow had been gathered and pooled.

The waterfront was crowded with almost all of the islanders who could walk, and even some of those who couldn't: residents of the home for the aged were propped against the steps of houses that faced the harbor. There was a group of the naturally outcast, the lepers, and they stood near the sea wall, defiant and proud, licensed by space, tolerated because they kept their distance. None had more than a slight rash. The other cases, those with ragged stumps and mummy-case skin, had the propriety to deny the carnival a collection of freaks. The fireworks could be seen from the colony.

In a circle of onlookers there was a line of dancers, young

men and women, each coupled to the next by a scarf. It was an old custom and was required by a morality so strict as to forbid even the innocent contact of fingers. The band was composed of a few cherished instruments; the screeching of violins, mandolins, and bouzoukis was amplified by the war's public-address system. There was a singer, too, and the words and the music and the dance had the tone of both unexplained loss and gladly accepted joy, a spirit that could absorb and was tinted by vanished boats, unrecovered bodies, matches made. No one could say the emotion was pleasant or painful: the atmosphere was graced by a buzzing and gut-sinking quality, an orgasmic knowledge of the mixture of success and failure.

Boot drank and watched and looked farther down the waterfront and saw Vaggelis' carnival.

"Look," said Costas.

Boot turned. Costas, Pavlos, and Petros had been standing behind him, had been watching the dancers as well.

"There's been a mistake," said Costas.

Boot looked at the dancers, listened to the music, and said, "I'll bet."

"What will you do?" said Costas.

Boot shrugged.

"Look," said Costas, "there's . . ."

"You told me," said Boot. "Where can I buy a bottle?"

"Up the street," said Pavlos.

Boot's eyes drifted over the stores.

"I want to speak for all of us," said Costas.

"What's stopping you?" said Boot.

Boot looked at them and laughed. Their terror was as brittle as glass.

"The carnival will be enough," said Costas. "It's time to forget, to enjoy yourself."

"Is that all?" said Boot.

"We were wrong," said Petros. "It's bad luck, but I should have taken the body, and we should have bought a new jackass, and you should have done nothing at all. We were wrong and angry because a foreigner did what we should have done ourselves. You're lucky we didn't kill you."

"Yes," said Costas.

"You're frightened," said Boot.

Costas nodded.

"We had two warnings," said Petros. "Once before and one today."

At least he delivers.

"So," said Costas, "speaking for all of us, I want to apologize."

Costas offered his pale shopkeeper's hand. Petros slapped Boot on the back. Pavlos smiled.

"Give me fifteen hundred," said Boot.

Costas was left with his hand in the air.

"It's cheap enough," said Boot.

"And you'll do nothing?" said Costas.

Boot looked down the waterfront, toward the hotel.

"More than that," said Boot. "I'll tell you what I was going to do."

The conference was held in the air, in the eyes alone.

"You've brought money for the carnival," said Boot. "Aren't you going to have your palm read?"

Petros frowned, but then laughed and elbowed Boot in the ribs.

"The old chickens have the best juice," said Petros.

"I'm sure," said Boot. "Count it out."

They counted it out.

"Good," said Boot.

"Well?" said Costas.

"Just this," said Boot.

He put the fifteen hundred in his pocket and walked toward the carnival. The bottle spun in the air: a spot on the colored surface of the water broke and heaved. Boot put two hands on the curb, kneeled, and vomited. The fluid was warm, comprising organic juices, liquor, and pinkish flesh. Boot slipped in it once, swore, wiped his face and hands on his shirt, and walked into the store and bought two bottles. His presence was scarcely noticed: the shop was crowded and everyone was drunk. The shopkeeper filled pots and jugs with wine from a wooden cask that was eight feet in diameter. The store was filled with the odor of sweat and pine resin.

Boot watched an endless piece of varicolored silk being pulled from a fist. A bird popped from a hat. Water turned to plaster: it wasn't late enough for orthodoxy. Boot saw blood, as bright and shiny as congealed wax, on the front and sides of the magician's cape. Foreheads swelled. Jaws sagged. Laughter and applause ran through the crowd. The magician pulled a dead rat from the cuff of Boot's pants.

The strongman twisted a nail into a corkscrew with his teeth, bent an iron bar over his head, parted the links of a chain that had been wrapped around his chest.

The acrobat turned a flip and landed on the strongman's stomach.

Vaggelis and the opium smuggler sat next to each other on the sea wall. Vaggelis' paunch was so large it rested on his thighs.

"You should get something to eat," said Vaggelis.

Boot looked at the acrobat, who was now turning cartwheels so quickly he looked like a pinwheel.

The opium smuggler said to Boot, "She's at the hotel."

The geek sat next to Boot's shoes, gazed at him with that same mild and engaging quality. Bugs crawled in the geek's beard, and Vaggelis took one and stuck it into the geek's mouth, and the geek chewed without concern, as though Vaggelis had given him a piece of tasteless candy. Vaggelis laughed and kicked the geek, who rolled once and then stood next to Boot.

"Go on," said the opium smuggler. "The carnival lasts all night."

The geek had performed for the first time: alcohol made the diseased patches on his face as red as a scarlet birthmark.

"You didn't do badly," said the opium smuggler. "For a foreigner."

"Yes," said Boot. "But your help is expensive."

The opium smuggler smiled and said, "It always is."

"Look," said Boot. He pulled the bank notes from his pocket. "I clipped them for another fifteen hundred."

"Fifteen hundred," said the opium smuggler, as though Boot were speaking of a losing soccer team. "So you're still trying."

Boot walked toward the hotel, moved along the crowded quay, was greeted and thanked for bringing the carnival.

"The time of my life," said a farmer. "The time of my life."

He drank from a jug, laughed, and was obscured by the crowd.

The high wire ran from a veranda on the second story of a house to a standard by the sea wall. The street was scaled with upturned faces, and each was brightened by the dusty illumination of a spotlight: the high-wire man was sitting on a chair with his bar across his knees and before him there was a table set with silverware, a plate of macaroni, and a glass of wine. There was a napkin in his lap. Boot stumbled against the standard. The high-wire man stopped eating. He looked like a diner who had felt the first tremor of an earthquake and then he was still, so quiet that his lack of movement seemed photographic, or more than photographic, since it was as though his stillness were a sponge that absorbed the slight vibration of the wire. He sat with his wineglass in one hand, halfway between table and mouth, and waited, and when the tremor was gone he looked at Boot and said, "Don't be clumsy."

The crowd laughed.

Boot climbed the stairs and banged on the door.

"What do you want?" said Mara.

"There's a carnival," said Boot.

He walked into the room and sat on the bed.

"I can hear," said Mara.

Boot put a hand against the wall. The violins squawked in the street.

"You're drunk," said Mara.

Boot shrugged, reached for the bottle, caressed the sheet, heard something scurrying under the bed.

"Christ," said Mara. "You should have stayed home."

"They apologized," said Boot.

Mara sat opposite him and drank from the bottle.

"What are you going to do?" said Mara.

Boot opened his empty hands.

"Do you want me to apologize?" said Mara.

"No," said Boot. "Why don't you come on down? Down to the carnival."

He walked through the door, down the stairs, and into the street. There were so many people in front of the hotel it was difficult to believe that a harbor was just forty paces away. Boot listened to the music, noise that seemed to come from the expanding and contracting stones of hell. The faces in the street looked as though they were being seen through an aquarium. Alcohol broke light into spectral colors. Fireworks filled the air. The cannon that shot them made a dull sound, as though Boot were standing next to it but had cotton in his ears. The air jarred against his skin. The fireworks bloomed against the stars, were reflected among the boats in the harbor.

Boot went into the palm reader's tent.

"You smell of vomit," said the palm reader.

"So what," said Boot.

"Nothing," said the palm reader. "What do you want?"

"Do you want to make some money?" said Boot.

The palm reader used her old whore's smile.

"Who doesn't?" said the palm reader. "But I thought you had a . . ."

"No," said Boot, "I don't. But that's not it."

"So?" said the palm reader.

"Vaggelis smuggles opium. It's going to be grown on this island. If you use that information carefully and don't get killed using it, you can make some money."

"I didn't hear you," said the palm reader.

"Think for a while," said Boot, "and maybe you'll hear me."

Without thinking or looking or in any way searching, Boot walked directly to a semicircle of people, a group that instinctively made way for him, stood back as though an eddied stench moved between them. Boot turned once and saw Mara, who looked at him and shook her head.

The geek said, "Here, geek."

Boot stared and shook his head and then even that last bit of resistance, that bit of habitual refusal, schematically the same as the twitching legs of the jackass after having run so far, was gone. Boot kneeled in the pen and the geek sat on its side and someone gave Boot a chicken. It squawked and Boot looked at liquid eyes and listened to the crowd, to the absence of any noise at all, saw Costas, Pavlos, Petros, Vaggelis, the opium smuggler, Mara. Boot bit the head off, tasted blood, felt his teeth severing tendons, breaking bones, the skull, tasted the bitter brains, broke the palsied beak, felt an eye burst: he swallowed and offered the geek's cup. His gaze was distant and steady, since he was now safe, in league with everything he had despised, having found immunity by relinquishing all that had made struggle necessary: honor, character, word, anger. *Now there is no one left and I'm not even curious whether it was a matter of loss or victory.* He offered the cup.